GRIM V...
OF HORROR

I climbed the slender spiral staircase to the top and found myself at the threshold of a large circular room completely surrounded with windows, creating the effect of a continuous wall of glass.

The room was empty. No footprints showed on the dusty floor, yet I had distinctly heard a sound coming from this room. Then I saw it . . . the shape of a man but without substance. It came toward me, gliding rather than putting one foot before the other, yet as it moved I heard the sound of its footsteps on the wooden floor.

It came until it stood directly in front of me and its face was that of a being beside itself with rage. I took a step backward and clung to the railing of the staircase. The figure raised its hands and I thought it was either going to strangle me—or push me down the stairs!

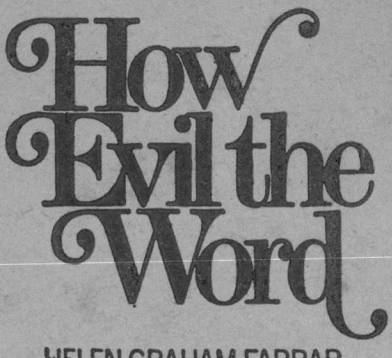

How Evil the Word

HELEN GRAHAM FARRAR

AVON
PUBLISHERS OF BARD, CAMELOT, DISCUS, EQUINOX AND FLARE BOOKS

HOW EVIL THE WORD is an original publication of Avon Books. This work has never before appeared in any form.

AVON BOOKS
A division of
The Hearst Corporation
959 Eighth Avenue
New York, New York 10019

Copyright © 1974 by Helen Graham Farrar.
Published by arrangement with the author.

ISBN: 0-380-00155-1

All rights reserved, which includes the right
to reproduce this book or portions thereof in
any form whatsoever. For information address
Barthold Fles, 507 Fifth Avenue, New York, New York 10017.

First Avon Printing, November, 1974.

AVON TRADEMARK REG. U.S. PAT. OFF. AND
FOREIGN COUNTRIES, REGISTERED TRADEMARK—
MARCA REGISTRADA, HECHO EN CHICAGO, U.S.A.

Printed in the U.S.A.

Dedication:

FOR ALMA AND HOLGER THORSOE WITH LOVE.

A word is dead
When it is said
Some say.

I say it just
Begins to live
That day.

. . . Emily Dickinson

How Evil the Word

Prologue

The child kept her eyes fixed on one of the fogged windows of the fire-lit study. Outside, sleety rain streamed from a slate-colored sky, flooding the bare flower beds, making fountains of Georgia red clay, and washing rivers of mud over the neat brick paths of the old-fashioned garden. The azalea bushes that would be so beautiful in the spring lifted wind-lashed branches and scratched noisily on the white-painted brick walls of the old house.

The child turned her head and looked from under her lashes at her father sitting in a brown leather armchair on the opposite side of the fireplace. Although the chair was deep and softly padded, he sat, as always, uncompromisingly upright, his back as stiff as that of a tin soldier. In his thin, freckled hands he held a newspaper, the print almost level with his eyes, huge and popping like a frog's, behind his thick-lensed glasses. She hated having to sit with him while he read the Sunday paper because she knew that although seemingly indifferent to her as usual, he was, in fact, aware of every squirming move she made and would tolerate them as long as she refrained from speaking. She longed for the courage to chatter, to incur his anger, to be banished from the room, a disgrace to be welcomed except for its additional penalty of one week without dessert.

There was an alternative and she chose it. At the moment when her father shook out the pages of the Book Review section which claimed his attention, she slowly and carefully slid down from her chair and tiptoed to the door. Once safely across the hall and on the carpeted stairs she let out the breath she had been holding; now, two flights to climb and she would reach the attic, her secret refuge from the rest of the house, always cozy and friendly except when her father was home. Then it became like a stranger and developed dark corners and made loud, creaking noises in the night.

She shut the attic door behind her and put a chair in the middle of the room, standing on it to reach the electric bulb that dangled on a cord from the ceiling.

The cedar chest was just as she had left it the last time, the lid propped open with a pair of doubled-up tan kid gloves because it was so heavy for her small hands to lift. Now, bracing her legs, she pushed up hard and drew in her breath with pleasure as she always did at sight of the jewel-colored silks within. The dresses had belonged to her mother, she knew, because in the tinted picture that stood on her father's bureau her mother was wearing the same rose-pink silk that lay folded away here with the others. She took them out, one by one, stroking them and holding their faintly lavender-scented loveliness against her face.

After a little while her eyes strayed, as usual, to a small tin trunk pushed almost out of sight in a corner made by the sloping roof. She had often thought of opening it but had imagined that such a small trunk could not hold much of interest, certainly not yards and yards of stiff silk like these in the chest. Now, however, with a stirring of curiosity she went to the trunk and raised the lid. Inside were folded garments, men's clothing, though unlike any she had ever seen before. In wonder she looked at the fawn-colored coat that lay on top, at the embroidered silk vests and the shirts of fine, white material streaked and yellowed with age. Kneeling, she lifted them out and laid them on the floor beside her, exclaiming softly with pleasure at the gold buttons on the brown coat and the silver ones on the blue.

At the bottom of the trunk lay a rectangular package wrapped in heavy, ivory-colored silk. She picked it up and sitting back on her heels, tugged at the silk that shredded in her hands. Round-eyed, she gazed at the painting it had concealed, running her fingers over the canvas stretched on a wooden frame.

A stone house with a red tile roof standing on the summit of a high, green hill; a long flight of broad, white, ballustraded steps leading down the hill to a narrow, stony beach and an expanse of turquoise-colored water; a stone pier with two small white boats moored beside it, and, at a little distance, partly concealed by the slope of the hill and some small bushes, the roofless walls of a small fortress.

The child could not take her eyes from the picture. She felt that she could gaze on it forever and never tire.

Suddenly she heard her father's voice calling her. With guilty haste she tumbled the clothing back into the trunk, wrapped the painting in its tattered silk covering and pausing only to clamber on the chair and pull the cord of the light bulb, tiptoed into the hall with her new-found treasure in her arms.

Too late she saw that she could not evade her father, already at the foot of the attic steps. His eyes stared accusingly at her through his heavy glasses as he advanced until, standing on the step below, he stretched out his hand and took the picture. Never before had she seen such an expression on his face, nor could she understand it, for never before had she come in contact with naked fear.

For the rest of the day her father kept to his room. Relieved by his absence, the child ate her dinner with the housekeeper and at bedtime tiptoed silently past her father's door.

When she dared to go to the attic again, she found that the key that had stood in the lock for as long as she could remember was gone, and no matter how hard she pushed against the door it would not open.

Chapter 1

I was twenty-two years old when my father died.

We last sat together in the study on a chilly Sunday morning in March, a day not belonging to winter, yet with no hint of the balminess of spring.

He sat in his worn, leather armchair turning the pages of the Sunday paper, coughing a little, touching his chest now and then, looking up once to say in his dry voice, "Must be coming down with something," adding under his breath, "Perhaps, after all, I shall die peacefully in my bed."

The cold expressionless eyes, magnified by the thick lenses of his steel-rimmed spectacles met mine.

"It is not a good thing to live with fear," he said. "At least I have spared you that."

I wished, as I had so often wished before, that he had spared me also the knowledge that I was unloved and unwanted. Young as I had been, just turned six, when my mother died, I can still remember the awful sense of desolation that settled over me when I realized that so much love had died with her and I could expect none from my father to replace it.

Later, soothing the hurt, there had been Mrs. Abernathy, the widow of a former teaching colleague of my father's at the small southern college in Augusta where we lived. Warm, loving, and understanding, she came as a temporary housekeeper, and touched by my need for affection, had remained. Through my childhood and to this day she has been, as each need arose, foster mother, nurse, playmate, confidante, companion and friend. I soon shortened her name to Abby and so it has remained for me.

My father, contrary to his hopes, was not, after all, to die peacefully in his bed. The illness that had threatened on Sunday proved to be an almost fatal attack of influenza, but he survived it and in time was able to sit in a chair in a sunny window and doze over his newspaper.

One day, however, during the second week of his convalescence, Abby came to the study where I was typing the manuscript of my father's latest book.

"When did you last go to your father's room?" she asked.

I glanced up casually. "When I took him the mail at nine-thirty. Why?"

"That's over two hours ago and he hasn't rung yet for his eggnog. You haven't heard his bell, have you?"

"No, come to think of it, I haven't."

"You know he likes to think I have to be reminded of the eggnog so I humor him and wait 'till he rings, but he's never waited this long before."

"He's probably forgotten all about it. Go ahead and take it up, why don't you?"

"I'm worried, Alix. I wish you'd come with me."

We went upstairs, Abby carrying a silver tray with the glass of eggnog on it.

My father's door was open and I saw that he was not in the chair by the window. Too shocked to speak or make a move I stared at his inert figure sprawled face down on the rug, his legs at a grotesque angle like those of a runner halted in mid-stride, his arms outflung, both hands clenched. The letters I had taken to him earlier lay scattered on the rug. The ottoman on which he liked to rest his feet was overturned, and the silver bell for summoning Abby had rolled some little distance from the chair.

I heard the tray fall from Abby's hands and smelled nutmeg as the eggnog spilled from the glass. To this day the smell of nutmeg makes me feel ill.

Abby ran and knelt beside my father, turning his head so that his face was no longer crushed into the rug. Whatever it was that had struck him down must have come suddenly and without warning because his eyes, wide open and staring, showed terror as well as surprise.

"The doctor—quick, Alix."

When he came he pronounced my father dead and spoke regretfully of losing an old friend.

"Death was probably almost instantaneous," he said, rising awkwardly from his kneeling position beside my father. "He was alone, probably knocked the bell off the table and couldn't reach it. Realized he was going to die and was afraid. I am very sorry. Sudden death always comes as a shock."

"I can't believe it," said Abby. "He was so well until this attack of flu. He never even hinted at heart trouble."

"Heart was as sound as a bell," said the doctor. "Looks to me as if he'd had a shock of some kind. What about those letters? Anything unusual there?"

I picked them up and glanced through them.

"Nothing," I said. "Just circulars and bills."

Puzzled, I stared down at my father's face that was twisted in an expression of fear. He had not been one to display his emotions; in fact his students had nicknamed him "Old Stone Face." Never in my life had I seen him look like this—or wait—had I? In the back of my mind rose a hazy recollection of his face, younger, by far, than the one at my feet, but twisted into the same mask of fear. When had that been? I tried to remember, but could not.

During the days before the funeral I learned to my surprise that my father, always stern and taciturn at home, had had many close friends in the teaching profession and the world of literature. They sent masses of flowers and crowded into our two downstairs parlors on the day of the funeral. It was strange to think of my father as a social person. I had known him only as a silent, withdrawn man guarding his home from any unnecessary contact with the outside world. Yet now these men referred to him as "John" or "dear old John" and said that I must come out of my shell and meet some young people. My shell! Certainly it had not been of my own choosing.

On the way home from the cemetery I asked Abby the question that was often in my mind. I turned to look at her, loving as always the proud lift of her head and the promise of a smile that was never far from her lips.

"Did my father ever show any affection for me? Sometimes I seem to remember little things from long ago, like a game of hide and seek, or seeing him smile as he tucked me into my bed, but it's all so very hazy and, well, impossible, that I guess it can only be wishful thinking."

The smile came and her voice was warmly reassuring.

"You haven't imagined it, dear. Those things really happened. Your father was the typical middle-aged scholar who falls in love for the first time, marries and idolizes his wife and is almost overcome with joy when he becomes a father. My husband and I often visited your home and were delighted at the way he shed his years and became like a child when he played with you. Then, when your mother died, everything changed. I came as housekeeper and was told to keep you away from him except on Sunday mornings when you were to sit with him in the study." She reached out her gloved hand and patted my knee. "Poor little mite, how tired you used to get."

"I remember," I said.

"Well, that's the way it was. He denied you nothing and always insisted that you be provided with the best of whatever you required. His only demand was that you be kept out of his way, but in spite of that I never thought that he disliked you. When you finished college, he suggested a business course so that you could become his secretary if you wished. All he asked of you was efficiency and was glad to pay you a good salary for it."

"Hardly the portrait of a loving parent," I commented bitterly.

"Don't judge him too harshly, Alix. He loved your mother very deeply and when she died, especially under such tragic circumstances, he just shut love out of his life. After awhile he began writing and after the success of his first book he continued to write. Yet all the time I could see that he lived in fear of something."

"Fear?" I swung around to stare at her and the car swerved wildly. When I brought it back under control I asked more calmly, "Fear of what?"

"I don't know, except that once when he had pneumonia and was delirious, he raved about a curse on the Bonneys. He said he had been marked for death but because he loved his wife too dearly she had been the victim of the curse in his place. After he recovered he never referred to it again."

We drove in silence for a few minutes. Then I said, "Tell me again how my mother died."

Abby folded her black-gloved hands and rested them on her handbag.

"It was graduation day at the college," she said. "The diplomas had been given and the prizes awarded and the procession was filing out. Your mother had a seat on the aisle and as your father came beside her he paused and smiled and touched her on the arm. The person standing next to her was a student who had failed to get his degree because he'd flunked your father's course. The boy had been waiting for that minute and as your father paused he aimed a pistol at him. Your mother acted instantly and threw herself at your father, protecting his body with her own and receiving the bullet that was intended for him."

"And because of that he sentenced me to a life of loneliness." My voice was bitter. I felt bitter.

"No, Alix. I believe it may have been because he did not dare to love anyone again."

I spoke incredulously. "You mean you believe in that nonsense about a curse?"

Abby lifted her hands and let them fall back in her lap.

"Sometimes I do and sometimes I think, like you, that it is a lot of nonsense. All I can be sure of is that after your mother's death your father lived in constant fear."

I remembered, too, the many lonely years that should have been filled with love, the rebuffs to my timid, childish overtures of affection, the tears I had wept into my pillow at night.

Anger rose in me: my cheeks burned and my hands gripped the steering wheel fiercely.

"I've suffered enough through his superstitious fear of a mythical curse. I have a right to know why it made him reject me. If it's the last thing I do, I'm going to find out, I promise."

I kept my promise, but as things turned out it came very near being the last one I'd ever be able to keep.

The final sorting, filing or discarding of my father's papers was not a difficult task but with the passing of each day it became more tedious. He had been extremely methodical and had demanded the same of me in my position as his secretary. He was a professor of history and his concern with the past together with a growing interest in parapsychology had led him to visit the ruins of old houses in an attempt to resurrect the secrets that had died with them. His discoveries combined with a tremendous amount of research had led to the writing of five phenominally successful novels, and work on the sixth had been well advanced at the time of his death.

The manuscript and his notes were written in longhand with red ink on yellow second sheets, much crossed out and interlined and often almost impossible to decipher; so when I felt myself getting tense I'd put the work aside and go for a long ride, returning at sunset to drop in for a cocktail at the Country Club, where from the veranda I could see the white pillars of my house at the end of a short avenue of magnolias. Sometimes after the sun had set and darkness had obliterated the familiar surroundings, I found myself wishing to get away from Augusta, to travel, to meet people my own age, to make friends, and even, perhaps, to fall in love.

One morning, waking to gray skies and a pelting rain that stripped the azalea bushes and flung their blossoms like handfuls of confetti into a moist wind, I went, after breakfast, to my father's room to sort out his personal belongings.

The room had not been touched since the day of his death.

The picture of my mother in her rose-pink dress was on the bureau where it had stood for as long as I could remember. My face reflected in the mirror behind it bore little resemblance to hers—perhaps, I thought, if I had looked like her my father would not have found it so easy to withhold his affection from me.

I opened a drawer and looked at the little pile of monogrammed handkerchiefs and the rows of neatly rolled socks. To my surprise I found I was seeing them through a mist of tears and marvelled at the power of those small, inanimate personal things to level the barrier of un-love that had existed between my father and me.

Suddenly I wanted to be close to him, close in a way I had never been. I looked toward the chair in the window and at that moment I heard his voice as clearly as I had ever heard it during his life.

"Come here," said the voice. "There is something you must see."

I walked across the room, drawn as if by a powerful magnet, to the empty chair. It did not occur to me then to question the source of the voice or my ability to hear it—I simply did as I was told.

The chintz slipcover had been pulled away when my father fell from the chair and in the ensuing confusion neither Abby nor I had thought to put it right. Now, again automatically as if following instructions, I stooped and smoothed the folds of material into place, pushing it down as far as it would go between the seat cushion and the side of the chair. When my fingers touched a crumpled ball of paper that had been thrust deep into the hollow space, I felt no surprise—subconsciously I had known that it would be there.

I suppose that in every life there is an event or a thought upon which one can look back and say "That was the turning point in my life. Everything that has happened since then stems from that moment in time."

It has been so with me. I have never heard my father's voice again, but from the moment I first held the ball of stiff, crackling paper in my hand, I knew that my course was set and that I had no choice but to follow it.

I sat in my father's chair and smoothed out the paper ball on my knee. As it unfolded I found that it was composed of three items—a typewritten letter, a color photograph and a long, empty envelope in which they had been posted three days before my father's death. I did not recognize it as having been one of those I'd carried to him on that morning but that is not surprising since he had never wanted his mail sorted for him—pawed over, as he put it.

The letter, under the letterhead "St. Sebastian Historical Society, St. Sebastian, U. S. Virgin Islands," read:

"Dear Dr. Bonney:

"By the will of the recently deceased Brandish Pompineau of this island, his estate, 'Mon Domaine' becomes the property of the St. Sebastian Historical Society of which I am president.

"The chateau on the estate was built in the late seventeenth century by a French pirate, Jean Pompineau, who, when his ship was sunk by the British in our harbor, gained the protection of the corrupt governor of St. Sebastian, who provided him with a new ship in return for a share in all treasure to be captured on the high seas.

"Pompineau flourished and built himself a chateau richly furnished with loot from captured Spanish, English and East Indian ships. It has the added romantic flavor of a legendary curse, and the mystery of a barred room.

"Brandish Pompineau was, as far as we know, the last of his line and had lived for many years as a recluse. The circumstances surrounding his death are such that they may interest you, and you have shed light on many obscure events that transpired within the walls of ancient dwellings.

"It is the hope of the St. Sebastian Historical Society that you will accept the invitation we hereby extend to visit (at our expense) Mon Domaine, to live in the chateau, to absorb its atmosphere, penetrate its mysteries and finally, give the world another of your remarkable historical novels. All known, existing records will be made available to you.

"We shall be honored to have you accept our invitation.
    Sincerely,
        Jens Andersen, President"

I picked up the photograph and studied it—a large stone, two-storied structure with a conical tower at one side rising a story above the main section. From the summit of the hill on which it was situated a series of terraces, linked by a flight of wide stone steps, led down to a stony beach lapped by the small waves of an aquamarine-blue sea.

Puzzled, I placed my finger on a spot near the water where a thick clump of flowering bushes and vines tumbled in unclipped confusion.

"Behind this lies the ruin of an old fortress, a small one with a wide platform that was probably a gun emplacement. Now how in the world do I know that?"

I closed my eyes and pressing my fingers against them concentrated on an image of a house on a hill outlined against a bright sky; at the water's edge a stony beach and two small boats moored to a stone pier.

And then I had it, the memory that had eluded me—

a long climb to the attic, a small trunk under the eaves, a painting wrapped in fragile white silk.

I rose, and taking my father's key ring from the bureau where I had laid it, went with mounting excitement to the attic. The first key I tried fitted the lock. Inside the room I reached instinctively for the long cord attached to the light bulb: beneath it was the chair on which I had stood when a child. The cedar chest was still in its place, but the wadded-up kid gloves were gone and the lid was closed. Over in the corner was the little tin trunk. I knelt on the dusty floor and pushed up the lid, recognizing the fawn-colored coat, the bright silk vests, the fine linen shirts and the breeches. Probing deep, I found the rectangular package and taking it to the light, carefully unfolded the lacy shreds of silk that still remained. With the same breathless excitement I had felt as a child when first I gazed at the painting, I now looked from it to the crumpled photograph I'd brought with me and knew there could be no doubt that the house was the same. I turned the painting over and found, affixed to the thin wood backing, a piece of paper covered with writing in old-fashioned script and coated with clear varnish.

"This," I read, "is the curse that I, who choose to call myself Louis Bonney, did on the twelfth day of June in the year of 1829, place on my brother, on the faithless woman I loved and whom he had just married, and on the house that sheltered them:

"'On the souls of our murderous pirate forbears I invoke the curse of death by violence on you and your descendents down to the last of your blood line. I curse this house with hatred and strife and bloodshed for as long as its walls shall shelter one of your breed.' Then, overcome by my rage, I shouted the dreadful curse with which the Pompineaus have ever condemned their enemies to the torments of hell: 'Anathema Marantha!'

"Then he, with shaking fist upraised, did swear that for everyone of his that should perish by the curse, one of mine would die suddenly and without warning. My only regret is that I cursed the house I loved and upon which I have turned my back forever.

"To my descendents, should I ever be foolhardy enough to marry, I offer my apology for the grief I shall have knowingly brought upon them."

Glued below the document was an envelope addressed in my father's handwriting to "Alix." Inside was a letter headed "A Monday morning in March, 1955 when you are six years of age."

"My Daughter,

"Yesterday, doubtless to escape the boredom of my presence, you went upstairs to the attic where, to judge by the evidence of an open cedar chest and the rumpled state of its contents, you amused yourself by rummaging among your mother's dresses. Your curiosity also led you to investigate the contents of a small trunk under the eaves from which you extracted and tried to appropriate the painting which I found you holding in your hands.

"If, when you read this, you have any recollection of that day you will recall my agitation at seeing you with the picture. At the time you were too young to be told the story of the curse pronounced on the house and its inhabitants or to comprehend the reason for the fear that has haunted me for many years. However, I hope that after my death when you find this letter you will have attained the age of reason and will possess sufficient common sense to enable you to trace the descendents of Jacques Pompineau and ascertain whether the curse is still in effect.

"The small trunk has been in this house for more than a century and a quarter. My father told me it belonged to the first Bonney to settle in Georgia, our ancestor Louis, who built this house in 1839 for his bride. Nothing of his life prior to that date is known. The richness of his apparel and the excellence of his house indicate that he was a man of means and good taste. His life previous to his arrival in the then cotton growing center of Augusta was by his own choice a secret one. The location of his former home is unknown.

"Sudden, and often violent, death has wiped out all the known descendents of Louis Bonney except you and me.

"I believe that because of the great love I bore your mother, the death intended for me was deflected to her. For that reason I have stifled the natural love of a father for his child to insure that I, not you, shall be the next victim of the curse.

"You are the last descendent of a man who chose to marry and condemn his progeny to die, victims of the double-edged curse. Knowing this, have you the courage to search for the house that is pictured on this piece of canvas, to seek out any remaining member of the Pompineau family, to wait for his death, knowing that it will mean your own, to count the hours that remain to you? Or will you blindly accept your fate and live cravenly with fear as I, your father, have done? It rests with you.

"One last word: if, some day you discover in yourself the same strange gift which I have kept secret, that came to me unsought and which has brought me such fame and wealth as I possess, do not distrust or fear it, but accept it for what it is, a rare gift and granted to only a few.

Your father"

I do not know how long I sat there in the attic holding my father's letter. I do remember hearing the sound of my own voice saying for the first time words that can still fill me with wonder: "I am a Pompineau."

My father need not have worried about the course I would choose to follow. Today, as I write this, I can truthfully state that even had I known then the dangers that lay ahead I would still have made the same choice.

Chapter 2

The plane came in low over an expanse of turquoise water that, shading into green near shore, curled in creamy foam on a semicircle of glistening sand fringed with palm trees.

A smooth landing, gay music issuing from the loudspeaker a babble of voices, a burst of warm air from the opened plane doors and, bathed in sunshine against a background of emerald hills, a sprawling, white terminal building gay with animated groups of sun-tanned people in brief, bright tropical clothes—this was St. Sebastian as I saw it for the first time.

"It's incredible!" exclaimed Abby, shifting hands on her overnight case crammed with antique magazines and some paperback mysteries she'd bought at the Miami airport.

"Fantastic!" I agreed. "Everything is an exaggeration——the sky is too blue, the trees are too green, the flowers so gaudy they look artificial."

"Yes, even the people look different—as if they'd been roasted like coffee beans. I'm going to love every minute of this trip."

I laughed and tucked my hand into her free arm. "It's high time you had a vacation. Besides, you love a good mystery and Mr. Andersen's letter mentions three: a curse, a barred room, and the mysterious circumstances surrounding the death of the last member of the family."

"Right. But he left out the one that intrigues me most—the reason why Louis Pompineau became Louis Bonney. What could have happened to make him pronounce such a dreadful curse on his own brother, on a new bride, and even on the house he loved?"

"That's what I intend to find out. After all, he was my great-grandfather."

We were nearing the terminal and could get a closer look at the people behind the barrier. One in particular interested me: a small, slightly built girl a few years older than I, with shoulder-length blonde hair, startlingly blue eyes, a short, straight nose and petulant, brilliantly lipsticked mouth. Her skin was the color of coffee with cream whipped into it and was in sharp contrast to the chalk white of her brief shorts and halter top. Beside her stood a man whose height, while probably no more than six feet, was striking because of the proud way he held himself, like one accustomed to public recognition and accepting it as his due. I wondered about his profession. Was he an actor, a politician, a singer? He could well be any of them, I decided, with his air of self-confidence, those compelling dark eyes, sensitive lips, determined-looking chin and the thick, beautifully groomed hair with its amusing, eye-catching cowlick at the crown. The bronze perfection of his suntan was marred on one cheek by the thin, white line of a jagged scar that ran from eyebrow to chin.

As Abby and I approached the door of the waiting room, she sighted an unengaged porter and darted ahead of me, signalling for his attention. Involuntarily, I paused and glanced back over my shoulder. The man with the scarred face had turned his head and was watching me. His lips did not move, yet I could hear the words he was thinking as clearly as if they were voiced.

"Well, I'll be damned! Just when I'd about given up hope of finding her, she steps off a plane, walks past, then turns and looks at me, and her eyes are green, and her hair is like copper and she'd look like a doll in a hoopskirt. She is exactly right and—just my luck—will probably be gone before I get back. My plane's due in a couple of minutes but I can hardly walk up to her and say, 'For Heaven's sake don't go away until I get back,' can I?"

27

His lips twitched as if he were amused, and without thinking I smiled back. It's a wonder I didn't say, "All right, I won't."

The little spell was broken suddenly as a small, red-haired boy in green shorts and a white jersey catapulted himself against the man and clutched him around the knees.

"Daddy!" he shrieked. "Pictures!"

A young man approaching with a large camera smiled hopefully. "Just one?" he asked. "A family group?"

I turned my head and went to join Abby in the waiting room. The episode could not have occupied more than a flash in time for Abby's hand was still waving and the porter had obviously just seen it. I felt shaken by what had happened and followed absent-mindedly as he collected our luggage and called a taxi. The man was probably head of a Little Theater group, I supposed, and looking for someone to fill a certain part. I felt let-down.

During the ride into town, Abby exhausted her supply of adjectives suited to describe the beauty that unfolded before our eyes. Even the shabby little shacks beside the road delighted her because of the brilliant scarlet and purple bougainvillea draping the unpainted boards.

The hotel to which we were driven was on a steep hill overlooking the center of town and the harbor. It was the color of strawberry ice cream with vanilla trim and over the door, in black, were the numerals 1825.

As we climbed the steps that led from the street to the veranda a woman came from the front door, her eyes frankly appraising us as prospective guests. She could not have been more than an inch over five feet and her arms and legs were like matchsticks. Her hair, a downy, yellow fluff, was tied back from her face with a blue ribbon the same shade as her sharp little eyes. Her mouth smiled easily, the practiced smile of a hostess, but the chin below her mouth was square and rock firm. She could have been in her late sixties because her dry, wrinkled skin had the look of age on it, but her eyes, twinkling and, as I thought, a little malicious, made her seem closer in age to Abby who was in her mid-fifties.

She wore a white cotton shift with very large, bright red patch pockets and her bare feet were thrust into white vinyl scuffs.

The taxi driver, a burly fellow, black and shining as patent leather, set our bags down on the veranda.

"Brung you two guesties from de airport, Miss Gussie," he said. "Might be plannin' to stay awhile."

The wiry little proprietress looked from Abby to me. "How long?" she asked.

I opened my handbag. "That will depend on the outcome of a business call I must make. May I pay for a week in advance?"

Miss Gussie jerked her head at the taxi driver. "Set the bags inside and holler for Nero. He's somewhere around doing nothing."

In the office, a cubicle partitioned off from a dining-room-cum-bar, we registered while Miss Gussie, putting on the spectacles that hung on a silver chain around her neck, studied the entries.

"From Georgia, eh? My second husband came from Atlanta. I never did get to go there—only lived with him a couple of months."

A bent old native man came to the door with our bags.

"Take 'em to thirty-six and thirty-eight, Nero."

He shook his head dolefully.

"Yes, Miss Gussie, but why do it always have ter be de top ob de house? Ain' de secum floor jus' as good?"

"View," snapped Miss Gussie. "Besides, the climb's good for you. Limber up your bones."

The old man, grumbling, led us across the hollowed stone paving of an open patio, which was crowded with green-painted oil tins holding enormous green and red crotons and several varieties of hibiscus. Bougainvillea—a riot of magenta, scarlet, salmon pink and purple—clambered over the brick walls and hung in festoons from the galleries of the two upper floors.

Nero paused half-way up a flight of shallow, crooked stone steps and pointed to a bush of star-shaped white flowers.

"Cum night de jasmin smell real purty," he said.

We had been given front rooms at the top of the house. High above the town we looked over clustered rooftops to the harbor and the docks where a long, black freighter and three trim, white tourist ships lay moored side by side. On the opposite shore of the harbor, a long arm of land curved outward to the sea, rising from a gentle slope at the water front to a steep hill at its furthest point. On its summit was the stone house of the picture with its tower at one end. An American flag floated from it and as I watched, a sudden gust of wind whipped it taut revealing a pennant rigged below it. Abby, standing at the other window exclaimed delightedly, "The Jolly Roger, as I live and breathe!"

Suddenly I felt as if a cold wind had swept into the room. I stared with revulsion at the sinister black flag with the white skull and crossbones on it, symbol of piracy on the high seas, of murder, of unspeakable cruelties inflicted on innocent persons. For the first time since I had read the letter inviting my father to St. Sebastian, doubt assailed my mind. Did I, after all, want to plumb the dark secrets of the family to which I now knew I belonged?

I took a long, steady look at the house that Mr. Andersen had called the chateau. The wind had dropped and the Jolly Roger hung limp on its mast. The conical tower looked as gay and charming as if it were part of a child's cardboard castle.

Ashamed of my momentary weakness, I resolved to let nothing stand in the way of my determination to spend some days and nights in the house on Mon Domaine. As a beginning Abby and I must go and see Mr. Andersen at once.

"Stay on main street until you come to the World Plaza," instructed Miss Gussie. "Turn in and keep going until you reach a pizza parlor. Across from it is a tobacco shop and a museum full of stuff hardly anyone bothers to look at—a pity, because Jens Andersen is an authority on island history. He's chock-full of charm—you'll like him."

The main street of St. Sebastian was like a circus midway. A steady stream of traffic jammed the road, horns blared, drivers shouted at each other, tourists in outlandish costumes blocked the narrow sidewalks while they took pictures of each other loaded down with bulging shopping bags. The very air was filled with the heady excitement of a spending spree of magnificent proportions. Shops filled with fabulous-looking merchandise marked at freeport prices lined the street. On one side, branching off, were steep, narrow roads climbing to the pastel-colored houses that clung to the hillside. On the other, several alleys gave access to the waterfront. One, more pretentious than most, had a pair of iron gates at the entrance with the sign "World Plaza" and over it a fan of flags of many nations. I turned in and found the pizza parlor lodged between a flea market and a gourmet shop. Directly opposite was a high arched doorway framed in scarlet bougainvillea. Two iron doors were folded back against the gray stone walls, one bearing the inscription "St. Sebastian Historical Society and Museum"; and on the other, within a circle of brightly painted national flags, was the word TOBAK.

"Goddag!" The voice was warmly welcoming.

The man who had come from inside to stand in the doorway was, I guessed, in his late fifties. Unlike the casually dressed men I had passed on the streets he wore a short-sleeved shirt, a handsome silk tie and beautifully tailored gray slacks. His face had the high color typical of most Scandinavians, his frosty white hair was cut short and brushed straight back, his eyes were blue and sparkling with pleasure.

"You come to see the museum, ja?" he smiled. "That is good. I will show you."

"Later, thank you. It is you we have come to see. You are Mr. Andersen?"

"Ja, I am he. I can be of help?"

I handed him the letter he had written to my father. When he finished reading he glanced at me inquiringly.

"I am his daughter, Alix Bonney," I said, "and this is my friend, Mrs. Abernathy."

He smiled. "Come in, come in. It is cooler inside. These old buildings have thick stone walls. Originally they were warehouses and often filled with pirate loot." His eyes crinkled at the corners as he added, "You are interested, like your father, in old houses and their secrets? That is good. You come to assist him, ja?"

As he talked he placed fan-backed wicker chairs near the door.

"Mr. Andersen," I said as we sat down, "your letter arrived on the day that my father died. He had read it, I believe, because when I found it the contents had been removed from the envelope."

"Dr. Bonney is dead? That is indeed sad news. I am sorry to hear it."

"It was a shock to us. He had been ill but seemed to be recovering nicely. I have to come to ask you to let me take his place. I have had no experience, I am not a history scholar nor have I ever written a book. However, I was my father's secretary and did much of the research for his books. I am familiar with his methods and share his interest in the motivations and behavior of people who lived in other centuries. For strong, personal reasons also, I feel an obligation to write this book in his place."

Mr. Andersen crossed one knee over the other and made a steeple of his fingers. "It is understandable that your father's unexpected death has upset you. It is also understandable that you wish to carry on his work. But the Pompineau story—"

He hesitated and seemed uncertain how to proceed.

"Yes?" I prompted.

"I think you should not involve yourself in it. The history of the Pompineau family is an unsavory one, full of violence and bloodshed. The house, itself, has a curse on it. This would have had little effect on your father who was experienced in this aspect of his search into the past, but for a young woman like yourself, alone—" He broke off, shaking his head.

"But she will not be alone," said Abby. "I've been with Alix since she was a child and needed me to look after her. She's long since outgrown that need but in this case I believe I can still be helpful. I'll stay with her in the house, of course."

Mr. Andersen hesitated. "So many terrible events have occurred under its roof—"

I interrupted quickly. "I am not easily frightened," I said, "and neither is Abby. I believe, as my father did, that old houses retain the imprint of certain events that have taken place in them and that these events sometimes become visible. The appearances are not harmful. It's only the fear of them that's dangerous. I think, too, that a curse exists only in the minds of those who want to believe in it. I certainly don't."

Mr. Andersen again shook his head. His expression said that he pitied me.

"You are young, Miss Bonney, and as you, yourself, admit, inexperienced. A curse is as much a reality as a blessing and as certain of fulfillment. The curse of the Pompineaus had to endure until the last of the line should have perished."

"You said in your letter to my father that Brandish was the last of that line," I reminded him.

A troubled frown creased his forehead.

"Ja," he said slowly. "The curse may have died with Brandish, but the evil it caused is still present in the house. I know because I have felt it. I am not psychic; on the contrary I am a most practical man. Yet when I enter the chateau I become conscious of disturbances in the atmosphere around me."

"Disturbances?" questioned Abby.

"Perhaps vibrations is a better word. The walls are permeated with evil."

His voice had dropped almost to a whisper. Abby leaned forward and spoke earnestly.

"Mr. Andersen, please tell us about the curse; whichever it is—fact or fantasy—it has an important bearing on the history of the Pompineaus. We have traveled many miles to discover and record the true story buried under a century and more of accumulated rumor, superstition and lies. We cannot turn back now."

Mr. Andersen's eyes twinkled with sudden amusement. "What very determined ladies you are! I see no reason why you should not unearth the secrets of that very unpleasant family as long as you conduct your investigations at a safe distance from the chateau. Well, then, these are the facts that led to the quarrel between two brothers and the curse that it precipitated."

He leaned his head against the high, fan-shaped back of his chair and closed his eyes for a moment. Then, raising his head and looking at us with a smile, he began with the ease of an accomplished raconteur to tell the following story.

"In the year eighteen twenty-eight, a penniless, and as it turned out a scheming, young woman named Christine Mercer came from Philadelphia to St. Sebastian to live with relatives who had offered her a home in exchange for her services as governess for their children. Although still attractive, she had lost the first freshness of youth and was, I imagine, desperately anxious to find a husband.

"At that time the only Pompineaus living in the chateau were two brothers, Jacques and Louis. Jacques, the elder by several years, was away much of the time on extended voyages in his trading vessels. During one of these absences, Louis, just out of his teens, met and fell in love with Christine, who, as it later developed, was less interested in him than in his wealth and social position. When Jacques returned he saw Christine for the first time and wanted her for himself. To get Louis out of the way, he sent him on a voyage that would take him to many ports, and lost no time in persuading Christine to marry him. In the meantime, Louis, anxious to return to Christine who had promised to wait for him, disobeyed his brother's instructions and cut the voyage short, returning unexpectedly on the very day of the wedding. The drawing room and ballroom were filled with guests and the champagne was flowing freely. Infuriated by his brother's duplicity and Christine's infidelity, he snatched up a glass of champagne, and after cursing them and all their descendants, drained the glass and smashed it at their feet. Jacques then hurled his own curse at Louis, who rushed from the house, returned to the ship which had not yet begun to unload, and sailed away, never to be heard of again."

I thought, with a shudder, of the picture and the words written on the back of the canvas.

"The exact wording of the curse is not known," continued Mr. Andersen. "As is usually the case where there are several witnesses to an event, the guests gave different versions. All agreed, however, that Jacques' words had exacted 'an eye for an eye and a tooth for a tooth.'"

Abby and I exchanged a quick glance.

"So," she said, "wherever Louis went, he was pursued by his own curse."

"Ja, until the last trace of the union between Jacques and Christine should be erased."

Erased, I thought, by a single word. As ancient and evil as sin itself, the word *curse* had reached out through the years and touched the lives of countless innocent victims, my father and mother among them.

With all the pent-up resentment of my unhappy childhood I hated Louis Pompineau for what he had done.

Abby's voice broke in on my thoughts.

"Mr. Andersen," she was saying, "do you have any objection to taking us through the chateau?"

"On the contrary," he answered. "I was about to suggest it. Would you like to go tomorrow, in the morning, perhaps, before the sun gets too high?"

"We can be ready at any time you suggest." She turned to me. "Can't we, Alix?"

My spirits lifted at once.

"Of course!" I agreed.

It would be at least a step toward my goal.

"At nine-thirty, then," he said. "I will call for you."

As he took leave of us he brought his heels together with a sharp little click and bowed slightly from the waist.

Outside the shop the plaza was ablaze with sunshine and humming with activity. When we reached the gates we looked back.

Mr. Andersen was standing in the doorway of his shop, the brilliant scarlet blossoms of the bougainvillea like a picture frame around him.

Miss Gussie was right. Jens Andersen was full of charm and I liked him.

But, I added to myself, I was not going to let him prevent me from staying in the chateau on Mon Domaine.

Chapter 3

Under a blue, cloudless sky the harbor lay as still as a pond; a cluster of small sailboats with white sails set to catch the breeze appeared like water lilies scattered over its surface. In the wake of our launch thousands of tiny bubbles hissed and, bursting, showered us with cool spray.

"The boat race today is to St. Croix and back," said Mr. Andersen. "See that long, purplish shape on the horizon? On a day like this St. Croix can be seen very clearly. Ah, here comes the Goose, right on time."

On our right, taxiing over the water, was a seaplane. It paused briefly as if to catch its breath, and then with a roar of the motors sped toward the mouth of the harbor, rose and gaining height steadily, headed toward the horizon and the dark outline of the island of St. Croix.

Mr. Andersen pointed the prow of the launch toward the arm of land that was Mon Domaine. As we approached the shore, he maneuvered the launch to the side of a pier where a smaller boat with an outboard motor was moored.

A tall, powerfully built, light-skinned native who had been watching our approach stepped to the edge of the pier, caught the rope Mr. Andersen tossed him and knotted it through an iron ring. Then, steadying the boat, he helped Abby and me up onto the landing.

"This is Darwin," said Mr. Andersen stepping up beside us. "He and his wife, Delfina, served Brandish Pompineau for several years and have stayed on as caretakers of the house and grounds. Darwin and two other strong young fellows like himself are doing a fine job with the gardens. Delfina cooks for them and looks after the house."

Darwin grinned self-consciously.

"We does our best, sir," he said.

"What will the Society do with a big place like this? Rent it, perhaps?" Abby asked.

"No. We have decided that if no claimant appears within twelve months we will throw the house and grounds open to the public as a tourist attraction."

A claimant? Until this moment I had not seriously thought of myself as such. I felt a little thrill of excitement as I looked around me.

"We have to consider the possibility that Louis Pompineau settled somewhere, married and had children," he continued.

I did not have to try and recall the words that my great-grandfather had written. I knew them by heart:

"To my descendants, should I ever be foolhardy enough to marry, I offer my apology for the grief I shall have knowingly brought upon them."

This, then, was my domain, should I wish to claim it. A heritage of guilt and grief for me who had already had enough unhappiness because of it.

Darwin pointed to a jeep that was parked at a little distance.

"Dis way, please," he said and went on ahead.

Abby's pumps sank into the sand and Mr. Andersen quickly took her arm to help her. She was looking especially pretty, I thought, in her sheer lettuce-green dress, her short, gold-blonde hair still untouched by gray, feathering in the slight breeze.

At our left, leading up from the shore was a narrow path, rocky and partly obscured by weeds.

"The original approach to the chateau from the landing," exclaimed Mr. Andersen.

"How steep!" said Abby. "I wouldn't like to climb it, especially in these shoes."

"A little further along the beach is a newer path with steps that rise in easy stages and benches where one can sit and catch one's breath. There used to be another approach between the fort and the chateau, probably used by the pirates who came ashore at that point, but it is now so overgrown that it is impassable. Today the only means of access to the island is by boat, but formerly, when this was a peninsula instead of an island, there was a good road between here and St. Sebastian. It is no longer in use except for the section that lies between here and the chateau."

"Why was Mon Domaine cut off from St. Sebastian?" I asked.

"To create a channel for small craft. This suited the Pompineaus because after the tragedy of Claire's disappearance, they did not welcome visitors to Mon Domaine."

"Claire?"

"Jacques' daughter. It is said that he loved her more than anything in the world, more than his treasures of gold and jewels. She was, as the saying goes, the apple of his eye. Then one day when she was sixteen years old she disappeared. No explanation was ever found and to this day it remains a mystery. Jacques was almost demented with grief. He had bars put on her door; refused to see visitors and was never again seen in public."

"Poor man!" said Abby. "But," she added, "why weren't the bars removed after his death? Surely his heirs would have wished to open the room?"

"Jacques took care of that in his will with instructions that the bars remain until the death of his last legitimate descendant."

"Brandish," I said.

"Yes, of that we are sure."

Darwin was waiting for us and we climbed into the jeep. During the ride to the top of the cliff Mr. Andersen drew our attention to the clipped hedges of hibiscus that bordered the road. Heavy-headed blossoms, single and double, in a wide variety of colors swung on their delicate stems among the dark green leaves like ornaments on a Christmas tree.

At a word Darwin brought the jeep to a stop at a bend in the road. Before our eyes was a panorama of sea flashing in jewel colors under a dazzling sun—turquoise deepening to cobalt with small islands scattered over the surface like emeralds set in knobby bits of black onyx. Below, on our left, were the crumbling walls of the fortress. Above, on our right, the chateau perched like a great white bird on the pinnacle of the cliff. The fairy-tale tower with its pointed red-tiled roof, faced the sea with latticed windows on the first floor and shuttered ones on the floor above. Encircling them was a line of large square windows fronted by an iron balcony.

My eyes went higher to the sinister black emblem that on the previous day had filled me with misgivings.

Following my gaze, Mr. Andersen said, "The family chose to flaunt the symbol of their original profession. We've decided to continue the practice, thinking it may intrigue the tourists. The family's later interests, such as smuggling and the slave trade were also profitable but far less spectacular."

We drove on. The road ended in a sweep of crushed coral at the front of the chateau. Below the road a flight of broad white steps descended a series of terraces with benches placed where one could rest and enjoy the magnificent view of the sea.

At our right two wide, shallow steps led up to a pair of iron gates flanked by stone urns filled with luxuriant, red-leafed foliage. Fastened back to the wall with iron hooks were heavy wooden storm doors blackened with age.

All awareness of the present and the existence of my companions left me as I stared at the gates that stood between me and the compounded essence of wickedness, hatred and fear that I had determined to penetrate. As Mr. Andersen pulled open the gates my eyes went above them to a plaque of polished stone on which, deeply carved into the surface, was the emblem of a fleur-de-lis. There was nothing in the simple design to inspire fear yet I felt it, like cold, wet fingers on the back of my neck, crawling like some clammy, repulsive beetle down my spine. My body clamored for flight but my will drove me on and into the chateau.

We stood in a loggia with lofty ceiling and pointed arches through which we could see an open court and beyond it another loggia with wrought-iron gates like those through which we had entered.

In the center of the court stood a fountain that must once have been beautiful. A pink marble base, grimy with the dust of years, supported the bronze figure of a peacock whose wide-spread tail was fitted with rusted and broken nozzles. Scattered about were several small ornamental tables and chairs to which remnants of white paint still adhered.

At either side of the loggia a pair of wrought-iron gates swung open on their hinges. Passing through the one on our left we entered a foyer furnished with a console table, a mirror and a rich oriental rug. In one corner, a narrow spiral staircase led to the floor above. Opening a door in the opposite wall Mr. Andersen stood aside for us to enter.

"You are now in the tower," he said. "This is the library, above it is the room Claire occupied and over that is an observatory where the early pirate owners could stand and watch their ships come into port."

He touched a switch and a crystal chandelier hanging from a metal fleur-de-lis in the center of the frescoed ceiling sparkled with sudden brilliance and threw tendrils of rainbow-colored light to touch each object in the room. Groupings of chairs and small divans covered in faded gold brocade stood on an oriental rug that covered the entire floor except for a light parquetry border about two feet in width.

Mr. Andersen stooped and folded back a corner of the rug to reveal a pattern of fleur-de-lis that repeated itself, marching in precise rows like iris in a garden.

"In Claire's time one of the slaves who was skilled in working with wood laid new floors throughout the house."

Placed near a French window that opened on a garden was a rectangular writing table elaborately carved and gilded. Two matching chairs with high back and seat cushions of gold brocade with long, heavy tassels at each corner were drawn up beside it facing each other. Touching one of them Mr. Andersen said, "This is where Brandish was sitting when he was attacked and killed. He was struck down with the traditional blunt instrument, in this case a crystal decanter, and then strangled with the cord of his own dressing gown."

Abby shuddered. "What a terrible way to die! Were there no clues to the murderer's identity?"

"None. He came by night and probably entered by the French window which, according to Delfina, was usually open because Brandish seldom left this room. He was a poor sleeper and sat here until dawn or until the decanter was empty. The natives, who love nicknames, called him 'Brandy.'"

"Brandy," I thought, "Brandy, my cousin."

I went slowly to the table and touched its gilded elegance with my fingers.

Instantaneously I found myself looking at the figures of two men, where less than a second before, there had been nothing but a bare table and two empty chairs. One of the men, dressed in a red silk dressing gown, was leaning far forward over the table, his face apoplectic with rage. His hair, gray and unkempt, fell over his forehead and straggled in long, roughly shorn locks over his collar. His cheeks were covered with a stubble of beard.

The other, of whom I could distinguish nothing more than a hazy suggestion of a slim, tensed figure, kicked his chair from under him and leaped to his feet.

The man in the dressing gown cried out in a hoarse, choked voice, "Liar! Cheat! Over my dead body! Do you hear? Over my dead body!"

Suddenly his expression was transformed from anger to sheer horror. His body became rigid, his eyes, wide and staring, fixed themselves on a heavy decanter, which, clutched in steely fingers, rose quickly then fell with deadly accuracy upon his grizzled head.

I stood transfixed, every detail of the terrible scene imprinting itself on my mind even as the picture faded and dissolved before my eyes until nothing remained but the table and the two empty chairs.

Terribly shaken, I gripped the edge of the table and fought the nausea which turned me cold and sick almost to the point of fainting.

Was this, I thought, the strange gift of which my father had spoken in his letter? A rare gift, he had called it, granted to only a few. To me, at that moment, it appeared a dreadful affliction, a disease of the mind that could destroy one's reason. How long could I endure to hear unspoken thoughts, to listen to words uttered by the dead, to be a witness to an unspeakable past? With all the strength of my will I repudiated the unsought power that had come to me. I closed my eyes and waited for the dizziness to pass.

Mr. Andersen was still speaking.

"A chess board had been knocked off the table, the jade and ivory pieces scattered over the rug. Two wine glasses had been broken and lay a little distance from the table. The crystal decanter lay beside Brandish's chair."

I turned away from the table. "I thought he was a recluse," I said.

"So did everyone. That night, however, he had a visitor."

Abby asked, "What about Darwin and Delfina or the two gardeners? Didn't they hear anything?"

"No, they said not. They do not sleep in the house but have their quarters over the old carriage house. After the evening meal everything was locked up except for this room."

"Didn't any suspicion fall on them?"

"At first, yes, but all were able to clear themselves. Luke and Ben, the helpers, had been in town and were seen in several bars. They did not return to the island until after dawn. Darwin had cut his foot that day with a machete and was unable to walk. Delfina got up once or twice in the night to give him aspirin but said she heard no sound from the house."

"Were there no clues at all here in the room?" I asked. "Fingerprints, perhaps?"

Mr. Andersen smiled. "Our local police are not familiar with modern methods of detection. By the time detectives arrived from the mainland everything had been handled many times. Come," he added, "let me show you the rest of the downstairs rooms. There is another entrance to the tower on the floor above."

Back in the foyer we passed through an arched opening into an arcade.

"As you can see," he said, "the chateau is constructed around a square, open court with a loggia at front and back and an arcade at each side giving access to the rooms. We are now in the west arcade."

He opened a door that was ornamented with a gilded garland of fruit and flowers. The gilding was dull and the once-white paint on the door was dark-ivory and peeling badly but the effect was still elegant.

The room inside was shuttered and musty-smelling, filled with ghostly shapes of furniture swathed in dust sheets.

"The reception room," he said.

He lifted the edge of a dust sheet revealing a charming little chair upholstered in faded, rose-colored satin.

Abby touched it almost reverently.

"This belongs in a museum. It must be priceless."

"The house is completely furnished with antiques. On several occasions I have come prepared to catalogue them but found it impossible to remain long enough to accomplish much at one time. There has always been a sensation of the walls closing in on me and of eyes watching my every move. I am chilled—my scalp prickles—I want to get out of the house as fast as possible."

Turning to Abby he asked, "Do you feel it, too?"

She shook her head. "Why, no. The air is stale in here and there is an odor of mildew but that is to be expected. I haven't noticed anything else."

I was glad he did not ask me. I was shivering with cold and close to the edge of unreasoning fear and I would have had difficulty in dissembling. As long as there was even a faint hope that he could be persuaded to let us stay in the house, I must remain outwardly calm like Abby.

Next to the reception room was a magnificent staircase of white marble and beyond it a ballroom opening on to the rear loggia. Passing to the east arcade, we paused to peer into the dim interiors of a music room, a banquet hall and smaller dining room, a large pantry with a dumb waiter and a service room with a flight of steps leading to the kitchens on the floor above.

"Now for upstairs," said Mr. Andersen. I felt sorry for him because he was so obviously uneasy, turning his head from time to time as if he expected to see something or someone behind him.

On the staircase he pointed to a faint discoloration on one of the steps.

"That is where Jacques' wife, the ambitious Christine Mercer from Philadelphia, struck her head when she fell to her death, the first victim of the curse. It happened at a ball to celebrate the christening of her second child, Claire."

The first victim, I thought, shuddering. Was my father

really the last? I am the only living descendant of Louis Pompineau. Will the curse claim me, too?

At the top of the staircase was a pillared gallery surrounding the open court. From it one could enter the various rooms which, as on the floor below, opened into each other. All on the west gallery were closed and shuttered, but as we opened the doors we saw by the light from the gallery the swathed shapes of massive beds, wardrobes, dressers, chests and the smaller outlines of chairs and tables.

On the east gallery, which was reached by way of a service passage, the doors were all open and the rooms flooded with sunshine. Rows of gleaming copper pots and pans hung on the walls of an enormous kitchen. In the pantry the walls were lined with glass-fronted cabinets filled with sets of china, each in a different pattern. Shelves of crystal stemware ranging in size from tiny liqueur glasses to tall, stately goblets winked and glistened in the sunlight. One section of a wall was occupied by chests of drawers each, explained Mr. Andersen, containing sets of linen fit for a king's table which, he added drily, had probably been their original destination.

At the far end of the gallery, facing us, was the entrance to the tower. I was a few steps in advance of Mr. Andersen when suddenly my eye was caught by a movement in the shadows just within the doorway. A woman stood there in the half-light, one hand gripping the door jamb, her body inclined as if she were straining to watch us and overhear our conversation. In the next instant she sprang back into the room, moving so quickly that I almost doubted that I had actually seen her, and yet a fleeting impression remained of a face with tawny skin and eyes like black, smoldering coals and of two swinging braids of long black hair. There had also been a momentary glimpse of a bright red skirt before she had whisked out of sight.

Behind me Abby and Mr. Andersen were talking enthusiastically about antiques.

I hurried ahead into the room where the woman had been standing.

Nothing stirred. I found a light switch and flicked it on. In the illumination from a small, pink ceiling fixture I saw that whoever had been there a minute ago had disappeared.

The spiral staircase! It linked this room with the foyer below and the observatory at the top of the tower. Which way had she gone, down or up? Why had she run instead of waiting here to speak to us? Surely, if she was Delfina—and who else could it be?—she had the right as a housekeeper to visit any part of the house?

It didn't make sense, but then, neither did it make sense for me to puzzle my head over anything so trivial.

And then I remembered her eyes. Black as coal and smoldering like two banked fires. Shocked, I realized that what I had seen in them was venomous, undisguised hate.

Why? Why should this woman whom I had never seen before and who, I was sure, had no knowledge of the reason for my visit to the chateau, display such unmasked hatred of me?

And why, after what I had seen in the library, should I wish to remain in this house exposed, as I would be every day, to the hostility of the housekeeper? Why not tell Mr. Andersen that I had decided to abandon the project of the book, and return to Georgia and the familiar routine of life in a college town?

In his letter my father had questioned my courage. He had asked "Will you blindly accept your fate and live cravenly with fear as I, your father have done?" And he had added the challenge, "It rests with you."

A precipitate departure from St. Sebastian would amount to an admission of cowardice which, though known only to myself, would be shameful to live with. I had come fifteen hundred miles to verify my unwanted identity as a legitimate, though unknown, descendant of a pirate and to prove the truth or falseness of a curse from which my father had tried to shield me.

If indeed, pirate blood ran in my veins did I not owe my dauntless ancestors the evidence that their courage lived on in me? I would stay then and face whatever peril lay ahead for me.

A sound from the room above drew my attention to the spiral staircase. If Delfina were up there I wanted to face her, to make it clear that I was a guest of Mr. Andersen and to search her face for any sign of the hate I had already seen there.

I climbed the slender spiral staircase to the top and found myself at the threshold of a large circular room completely surrounded with windows, creating the effect of a continuous wall of glass. It was here, I supposed, that Jean Pompineau had stood, scanning the horizon for ships to be plundered and sent to the bottom of the sea.

The room was empty. Wherever Delfina had fled to, it was not this room for there was no place in which she could conceal herself. No footprints showed on the dusty floor yet I had distinctly heard a sound coming from this room. Then I saw it, the shape of a man but without substance. It came toward me, gliding rather than putting one foot before the other, yet as it moved I heard the sound of its footsteps on the wooden floor. It came until it stood directly in front of me and its face was that of a being beside itself with rage. I took a step backward and clung to the railing of the staircase. The figure raised its hands and I thought it was either going to strangle me or push me down the stairs.

Why can't I move? I wondered frantically. Why can't I turn and run to safety in the room below? I saw—such a trivial thing to notice at a moment when death seemed imminent—that the apparition had a magnificent ring on its forefinger—a ruby, I thought. The hand was so close now that I could see the design on the gold setting—a pair of fleur-de-lis curved like a cup to hold the jewel.

"I will not close my eyes," I vowed. "If this is death I will look it in the face."

And suddenly there was nothing there in front of me. Sun poured into the room, and I was alone, gloriously alone and free of the terror that had almost made me a coward. Nothing had disturbed the coating of dust on the floor; no sound broke the silence.

"I will not be afraid of this house," I said firmly. "I am not afraid of you, whoever or whatever you are. If you are a Pompineau, so am I. I will find a way to stay in this house and I will find a way to break the power of the curse if it really exists. I am stronger than you because you are dead and I am alive. Hear this—I am not afraid."

I went down the stairs and I stood in the middle of the room under the little pink ceiling fixture and I felt as brave as the bravest Pompineau who had ever looked death in the face and conquered.

My great-grandfather had lived in this house and had probably been born in it. As a boy he had romped with his older brother in the open court where the bronze peacock stood in the pink marble fountain. I imagined him as he may have looked, a small, laughing boy with flushed cheeks and rumpled hair, racing with his brother down the long arcades from one loggia to the other, playing hide and seek in the spacious drawing room, hiding behind chairs and sofas, squeezing his small body into the wine cabinet of the sideboard in the banquet room, crouching, perhaps, in a cubbyhole under the marble stairs on which, years later, the false woman he loved was to fall to her death. Here in this house he had grown to young manhood. There had been no pictures of him in the Augusta house so I had no way of knowing what he had looked like, but he must have been intelligent to have been intrusted with cargoes of valuable merchandise to be sold in foreign ports. He had, naturally been in demand socially as an eligible and immensely wealthy young bachelor and it was probably at some dinner party or ball that he had met, and subsequently fallen in love with Christine Mercer. How jubilant he must have been when, at the end of the long voyage on which his brother had sent him his ship dropped anchor in the harbor and he jumped into the small boat that would take him to the landing place on Mon Domaine. How his heart must have leaped as the strains of music reached his ears! How that same heart must have broken in anguish as he stood in the doorway of the crowded ball room and saw his brother dancing with a radiant Christine resplendent in her bridal gown and veil! He had seized a glass of champagne and, holding it high, had cursed them and all their descendants until the last of them all should draw his last breath.

And now, more than a century later I, his great-granddaughter, stood in the charming little blue and white foyer, under the pink ceiling fixture and suffered, in sympathy, the pain that he had suffered as he dashed down the road that he had climbed so joyfully only a short time before, and manned the small boat back to the ship from which nothing as yet had been unloaded.

Where did he go? How did he make his living? Who were his friends? Who was the woman he married, the bride for whom he built the house in which so many years later, I was to find the painting of the chateau he had both loved and cursed?

Yes, he had loved the chateau and I would love it, too. By the power of that love I would drive the evil out of it. I hadn't the faintest idea how to go about it, but there wasn't a shadow of doubt in my mind that I could and would achieve my purpose.

The first step, of course, must be to obtain Mr. Andersen's permission for Abby and me to live in the chateau. This called for finesse and, if I was not mistaken, Abby's gentle persuasion would do more to overcome his reluctance than any arguments I could present. Once established in the house I could search for any sign of an entrance to a secret room even though I was inclined to think it unlikely that such a hiding place existed and even more unlikely that there was any treasure to be found.

My confidence which had been building up now began to sag as I thought of Delfina and the hate I had seen in her eyes. If I hoped to succeed in determining the truth or falsity of the curse, and in the event that it really existed, to drive it out of the chateau forever, I must discover the reason for Delfina's enmity and protect myself against it.

And what of the terrifying visions I had seen? Would there be other and perhaps even more fearsome ones in store for me?

In the last words of his letter my father had enjoined me not to fear or distrust the rare gift which, I now knew, had opened my eyes to visions of the past.

Was my courage strong enough to resist the fear-inspiring power of the supernatural?

Chapter 4

"My dear Mrs. Abernathy, you are very generous. But are you sure you wish to do this? It's a big undertaking, you know."

"Of course, I'm sure. With our combined knowledge of antiques we can make short work of a big job."

Their voices came to me from the gallery outside the door.

"Ja, that is true. Are you certain that you want to stay here with only Miss Bonney for company?"

Abby laughed. "I am never nervous. Besides, you will be here during the daytime to work with me on the inventory and at night there will be three men within call at the coach house. As for ghosts, I don't believe in them."

"Not ghosts, Mrs. Abernathy. It is the presence of evil that inhabits this house."

"What it needs then is a good airing. It probably hasn't had one for a hundred years."

"I see that I cannot convince you."

"Then it's setlted, isn't it?"

They came into the room. Abby's eyes were sparkling with excitement—she looked hardly a day more than half her age.

"You heard, Alix? We are going to live here in the

chateau. While you are busy with your book, Mr. Andersen and I will be cataloguing the contents of the house. I can hardly wait to begin."

"It's wonderful," I exclaimed. "I'm like you! I can hardly wait to begin. Thank you very much, Mr. Andersen."

"Not at all." He turned pink and looked as pleased as if our staying in the house had been his own idea all along and he'd just been waiting to surprise us with it.

Abby stood in the middle of the room looking around her. "What a lovely entrance room to the tower—it's charming."

Absorbed as I had been in my pursuit of the elusive Delfina I had taken no notice of the room except for the staircase—now I looked at it all with interest. This foyer to the tower was similar to the one downstairs except that the furnishings were more feminine in character. The console table was of some light-colored wood inlaid with mother-of-pearl. A Dresden china bowl with matching candlesticks stood on it and were reflected in an oval mirror framed with gilded cupids and garlands of flowers. The rug was cream and blue though much discolored by the dust of years. Placed on either side of an arched opening in the wall opposite the door was a small armchair upholstered in pale blue. Beyond, like an incredibly ugly painting in an exquisite frame was the door to Claire's room. Heavy beams had been nailed across it at short intervals hiding all but a glimpse or two of ivory surface and a few fragments of a gilded garland. I had been prepared for the sight of a barred door: what I now felt I looked upon was a man's heart broken beyond healing. All that remained to him of a beloved daughter had been shut away behind those bars—the little keepsakes she had treasured, the comb she had drawn through her hair, the dresses she had worn, now hanging in her wardrobe, still fragrant, perhaps, with the scent she had used. A flower fragrance for a young girl—rose, perhaps, or jasmine?

I could not bear to look any longer at the door. I wanted to tear the bars away, to burst it open, to let the blessed air and sunshine into her room. She had been so young, only sixteen, surrounded by love and beauty, wanting for nothing. What had happened to her? Where had she gone? Had her life ended tragically one terrible day and had her body been hidden away in the tower room? Or was she in some far-off place, lying in a lonely grave, far from the tiny island where she had been happy and sheltered? I felt a surge of love and pity for the little cousin who had lived and died so many years before I was born.

Reluctantly, drawn by an urge that was like a command, I stepped through the archway and laid my hand on the barred door. For one, breath-taking moment, then, I saw her. I could have reached out my hand and touched the coppery hair that fell on her shoulders in soft, loose curls. Her eyes, green like mine, with long, dark lashes looked directly into my face; her lips parted in a smile as if she were glad to see me.

And then she was gone. The proof of her presence was there, however, in the lingering fragrance of a perfume I could not identify, delicate yet sensuous, reminding me a little of the tea-olive shrub that grows in Georgia.

Why had she looked pleased that I had come? Was I not the great-granddaughter of that Louis Pompineau who had cursed her parents and all their descendants—and even the house where she was to be born, to live to young womanhood and finally—perhaps, to die?

Slowly the shock of seeing her lessened.

"Do you plan to open Claire's room or keep it a mystery?" I asked.

"We have decided to open it. You may be present if you wish."

I thought of Claire as I had seen her a moment before, her soft curls lying on her shoulders, her eyes smiling a welcome. Would we find her there behind the barred door, a little heap of bones and a skull as round and white as a lump of sun-bleached coral, a ring, perhaps, on one bony finger, a string of pearls still clasped around her skeleton throat?

Had she been, like so many others before her and so many who were to follow, a victim of the family curse?

I shuddered with loathing of my Pompineau blood.

I did not sleep well my first night on Mon Domaine.

Dinner was prepared by Delfina who, upon our arrival with Mr. Andersen earlier in the day had introduced herself briefly as the housekeeper, and was served by Darwin, immaculate in a starched white suit. Afterward Abby and I went to our rooms and settled down for the night, she with a paperback mystery and I with a notebook and pen. It was late when I completed my record of the day's events and locked the notebook in my suitcase with the painting of the chateau which I had removed from its frame and rolled loosely in tissue paper.

Of Delfina I had written: "She is tall and walks with the erect posture and gliding pace of those West Indian women who can carry a five-gallon tin of water on their heads without spilling a drop. Her hair is long and black and she wears it in two braids as thick as my wrist. Her heavy eyebrows meet across the bridge of her nose giving the appearance of a perpetual scowl: below them her eyes are black and baleful. For lack of a better word, her skin can be described as tawny, somewhere between brown and yellow very faintly tinged with pink. Her bearing is arrogant and her manner hostile. I shall leave all communication with her to Abby, for, frankly, she gives me the creeps."

The air was very warm. I turned out the light and felt my way across the unfamiliar room. At the window a slight breeze from the sea lifted my hair from my forehead and cooled my face. From somewhere in the darkness below there rose the fragrance of jasmine giving to the night all the sweetness stored up during the heat of the day. The only sound to break the stillness was a shrill, intermittent "co-kee" which I supposed to be the cry of a night bird, but, as I was to learn later, came from the throats of innumerable and incredibly small tree toads. Overhead the moon, bright as a new-minted gold coin, cast a shimmering runway of light on the dark water below.

Turning my head I could see another window fronting the sea, the shuttered window in the tower where, on some long-ago night like this Claire may have stood, lost, as I was now, in the magic of the subtropical night. Above, the moon was reflected in the glass windows of the observatory.

Acting on impulse I picked up my flashlight and made my way along the gallery to the foyer of the tower and climbed the spiral staircase which led directly into the observatory. The room was bright with moonlight and without bothering to look for a light switch I crossed the floor and stood at the window. As I had expected, the panoramic view of gold-spangled sea and a boundless sky strewn with myriads of colossal stars and a moon riding high over all was spectacularly beautiful. Below the tower the coral driveway that had been dazzlingly white under the sun now shone with a faint, blue tinge like a fresh fall of snow under a winter moon. Beyond lay the broken flight of white balustraded steps descending to the ruined fortress.

Suddenly the light dimmed, and looking up I saw a bank of clouds drifting across the face of the moon. Driveway, steps, shrubbery and sea, all were blotted out as if they had never been: only the faint outline of the fortress was distinguishable in the pall of darkness that fell like a great, black cape from the sky.

Down by the water something moved, a shadow against a faint illumination within the fortress. Startled, I watched as a yellow speck detached itself and advanced slowly, swinging in small, rhythmic arcs. Others followed, forming a procession of lights that mounted steadily up the old, disused path from the sea. A thin edge of the moon slid out from under the clouds and illumined the figure of a man standing on the grassy margin of the driveway at the point where it curved around the tower. Emerging from total obscurity into the shaft of moonlight, his figure appeared enormously tall and broad. His shirt was white and open to his waist, the sleeves rolled high on his powerful-looking arms and the black breeches he wore were stuffed into the tops of high, black boots. He raised his head and scowled at the sky, his bushy eyebrows and square-cut beard as black as the bandana that was knotted around his head. With pantherlike swiftness he whirled and swung his lantern once, twice, at shoulder level: instantly the other lights disappeared and a faint click of metal against metal came to my ears as the leader, clearly visible in the moonlight, closed the shutter of his lantern. I pressed my face against the glass and strained to see the file of dark figures that moved silently, close to the wall of the tower. A few were carrying chests between them, others had bulky sacks swung over their shoulders.

Suddenly in a burst of brilliance, the moon flung itself from the clouds that still partly obscured it, and soaring like a child's balloon released from restraint, flooded the sea, the fortress, terrace and tower with silver light.

But of the men I had seen with their lanterns and their burdens not a trace remained.

Could it possibly have been only a fantasy, I asked myself, a spell woven by the West Indian night? Or was it another vision like the one I had already seen, of a past to which I was irrevocably bound? For a moment I stood staring, unable to move and then, afraid to remain any longer in the room, ran to the stairs and still holding my flashlight in one hand, gripped the narrow iron handrail with the other for support. That was what saved me, for when the heavy blow struck my back between the shoulders I pitched forward, my body swinging by one arm, my hand locked around the rail. As I fell I let the flashlight fall from my other hand and wrenched my arm around until the fingers touched and fastened on the rail. Hanging there in the dark the full weight of my body on my arms, my legs dragging helplessly on the steps, I forced myself to stay quiet and to listen for any sound in the room above.

There was nothing but profound silence.

Carefully, I felt with the toe of my slipper for the step, got both feet on it and bracing myself against the rail drew my body upright. The flashlight had probably fallen all the way to the foot of the steps but I did not wait to retrieve it. Driven by an angry determination to find out who had tried to kill me I went soundlessly in my soft slippers back up the stairs to the observatory. The moonlight had not yet reached across the room to the top of the stairs and I stood there scarcely breathing, grateful for the concealing darkness. Someone was in the room with me, someone who wanted me dead. At the risk of another attack I had to see the face of my unknown enemy. If I could take him by surprise—I felt on the wall to my right for a light switch. It was there as I had hoped. As my fingers touched the metal plate I held my breath and flipped the switch. There was a sharp click, nothing more. Appalled I realized that not only had my presence now been revealed but also my exact location in the room.

My only chance to stay alive depended upon my gaining the bottom of the stairs before the steely hands that might even now be reaching for me could repeat their murderous attempt. This time, I was sure, they would not fail. I whirled, gripped the handrail, felt with my foot for the edge of the step and fled for my life. Midway down the stairs I lost one of my slippers and for a terrible moment felt my bare foot slide from under me. Again, as before, my grip on the rail saved me from falling. I had wrenched my arm, but although it hurt badly, I managed to hang on until at last my feet touched the rug on the floor of the foyer.

Something white stood between me and the door.

I froze, actually feeling the chill of the ice from which I seemed to have been carved. And then I saw that the figure was Claire.

I moved and she stepped aside to let me pass. She looked at me with an expression so full of sadness that I instinctively reached to touch her hand but she drew away. Keeping beside me as I ran along the dimly lighted gallery, she stopped at the door of my room and simply wasn't there any more. To say that she disappeared or that she vanished into thin air would seem to imply some sort of action on her part, of which there was certainly none. She simply was and then was not.

Shivering in the warm night air I turned the knob, went in and locking the door, made my way across the room to the bed, ghostly in its voluminous veil of white netting. All night I lay there alternately dozing and waking, seeing once again the line of lights snaking up the hill from the fortress, reliving the terror of my flight down the spiral stairs, looking again at the sweet, sad face of Claire. When at last the sunrise that filled my room with gold and crimson light, bringing the dawn-sounds of birdsong, jubilant cockcrow and the insistent barking of some distant dog, I rose and looked out on the rose-tinted sea. I could easily picture a pirate ship riding at anchor beyond the fortress, small boats pulling away from the side, ropes tossed up to hands ready and waiting to secure them to iron rings. Just so had Jean Pompineau's pirates come bearing gold and jewels to the chateau, treasure that might still possibly lie somewhere within its walls.

Turning from the window my eye was caught by something lying on top of my dresser.

It was my flashlight. Beside it lay the slipper I had lost on the stairs.

Last night I had locked my door and left the key in the lock.

It was still there; the door had not been opened. Yet there, before me, real to the touch of my fingers, lay tangible evidence of my flight from the unknown terror in the tower. By whose hand had they been retrieved and returned through a door locked against any intruder? Any, that is, except the friendly one who had no need for a key.

A warm feeling of security came with the thought that Claire was on my side against the forces of evil.

Then why, I wondered, had she failed to come to my aid in the tower?

Chapter 5

We opened Claire's room on a morning in early May. Gray clouds hung low over the hills and a misty rain blurred the outlines of three cruise ships moored at the docks across the harbor from Mon Domaine. Inside the chateau the rooms were steeped in gloom—even the courtyard with its newly scrubbed and polished tiles and the metal furniture glistening with fresh white paint looked dismal and uninviting.

There were five of us gathered in front of Claire's door: Mr. Andersen, looking very Danish with his bright blue eyes and fresh complexion and an air of authority that became him well; Miss Gussie, Vice-President of the Society and looking, in her state of excitement, for all the world like a wiry fox terrier straining at a tight leash; Abby, a little pale but not tense; and, standing beside me, a young man whom Mr. Andersen introduced as Jon Daley, owner of the local radio station and co-owner with his father of the St. Sebastian *Tidings*. I liked him the moment I saw him coming into the loggia behind Miss Gussie, smiling at me over her fluff of yellow duck-down hair.

He was tall and stout, but like many heavily built people, he carried his weight well and walked with a light and easy step. His eyes were blue and very alert, his hair dark and slightly inclined to wave, and his smile was warm and friendly.

"Miss Alix Bonney," he said, drawling my name after Mr. Andersen had introduced us. "I'm told that you come from my part of the world. It's good to meet a fellow Georgian so far from home. I was born in Atlanta, though I've lived here for a good many years."

"And never lost your accent," I laughed.

"I'm as Southern as ham and grits," he grinned and then added seriously, "You know, I often feel like getting away from all these palms and floppy-leaved banana trees and that damned ubiquitous hibiscus. I'd like to look once more at dogwood in the spring, see the redbuds popping into bloom, sniff the lemony smell of magnolias, hold a perfect camellia in my hand, listen to a mockingbird and watch the flash of a cardinal's wing. To put it mildly, Miss Georgia Bonney, I get powerful homesick at times."

Miss Georgia Bonney! I liked the sound of it. I liked the little feeling of homesickness, too, that it brought with it.

Now, standing at Claire's door, he had the keen-eyed watchfulness of a reporter on the trail of a good story. I could almost see him prick up his ears as the sound of footsteps came from the gallery and a minute later Darwin and Luke entered, each carrying an axe and a large clawhammer. They were strong, powerfully muscled men but their blows had little effect at first on the thick bars which seemed to resist every attempt to remove them. We stood in silence, each of us remembering, I suspect, that the house had a curse on it and wishing that we were anywhere else at the moment than in front of the sinister barred door. Slowly, very slowly, the great iron nails came out and the bars fell one after the other with the rending sound of splintering wood and the protesting screech of nails wrenched from their sockets. With a final blow of his axe Darwin smashed the old-fashioned lock and stood back from the door. At a nod from Mr. Andersen he and Luke went away, their footsteps loud on the gallery floor and the marble stairs.

The door swung open under Mr. Andersen's hand. The flood of sunshine pouring in through the windows took me by surprise although it should not have, because I had stood early that morning at the foot of the tower and watched as Darwin climbed a tall ladder that was steadied by the two gardeners and removed the heavy wooden bars from the massive storm shutters across the four windows of Claire's room.

Mr. Andersen entered first with Miss Gussie at his heels. Crossing the room, they unlatched the grimy casement windows and flung them wide. Instantly, caught in the draft between them and the open door, a small flurry of white down floated like snowflakes. As I stepped over the threshhold I was conscious of Claire's presence near me although she did not make herself visible.

We stood, a tight little group of five, searching the room with our eyes, each of us concealing beneath a mask of simple curiosity our individual hope, dread, or ghoulish anticipation of finding Claire's skeleton on the bed or on the floor or even crammed behind the doors of the huge wardrobe set against one wall.

The bed was a small, four-poster with a cornice from which still hung shreds of a thin, faded-pink material that could have been dimity. A ruffled spread of the same material hung to the floor in ragged strips. A pillow had split open and spilled its contents in a soft heap at the head of the bed.

Miss Gussie went to the wardrobe and tugged at the doors.

"They're stuck," she said over her shoulder. "Jon, come help me."

He got them open and we clustered around him while he ran his hands behind the dresses that hung inside on hooks.

"Nothing in here," he said. "The wardrobe must be airtight—the clothes are in excellent condition."

They hung there just as I had imagined them, light, flower-colored dresses trimmed with ruffles and lace and ribbon bows. I even fancied I caught a whiff of the fragrance that had reminded me of the tea-olive blossom. Above, on a shelf, stood a row of shoes and slippers so small that my own small feet would have found them a tight fit.

"She couldn't have been any bigger than I am," said Miss Gussie.

She wasn't, I thought, remembering the small figure that had walked with me from the foyer to my room.

"Come look at this, Miss Georgia Bonney."

I turned. Jon Daley was sitting on a cushioned bench at a dressing table set between two windows. In his hands he held a box made of the same light wood as the bed and dressing table.

"Pretty, isn't it? Take a look."

He stood, pushed aside the gold toilet articles on the dressing table and set the box down on its four short, square legs. It was a rather large box, about fifteen inches by eight, I guessed, and perhaps five or six inches deep. The wood had once been highly polished: set into the lid in darker wood was a fleur-de-lis.

Jon said, "Interesting, isn't it? I'd say it was made by the same man who did the floors. He was a child came to the island in one of the Pompineau slave ships to be sold along with his mother. The woman died during the voyage and the boy was brought to the chateau as a houseboy. He was about the same age as Jacques and Louis, the brothers who in later years were to have the famous quarrel that ended in the curse. He was bright and the family made a sort of pet of him—let him sit with the boys during their lessons and so on. He was devoted to the family but just about the time of Claire's disappearance he ran away."

"Was he ever found?"

"No, apparently Jacques just let him go."

"I wonder why. If he was such a valuable slave you'd think his owner would want him back."

"Well, Jacques had gone all to pieces about Claire, and besides, it was the time of the slave uprising on St. Croix. He was a bitter enemy of the Governor who wanted to free the slaves. All in all I suppose he couldn't have cared less about the loss of just one slave with so many other things on his mind."

He pushed the box nearer me. "Go on, open it."

Inside, on a pad of blue velvet, lay a number of rings and pins fashioned of small, but what appeared to be very good stones, in simple gold settings. Jon lifted a corner of the velvet. Beneath it, the wood was inlaid with another fleur-de-lis.

I've never been one to cry easily, but the sight of Claire's jewels, so unpretentious, treasured by her in a wooden box made by a devoted slave, brought tears to my eyes.

Jon offered me his handkerchief. "I'm glad we didn't find Claire's body here in the room," he said, "because this is the only handkerchief I've got with me."

Did I imagine it, or did I really feel the light touch of invisible fingers on my cheek? Was this another manifestation of the "rare gift" that I was beginning to dread and fear?

The others were moving toward the door. I was glad to go. I felt as if I'd been at the funeral of someone I loved.

In the foyer we waited while Darwin was summoned to put a padlock on the door.

Miss Gussie laid her little bird-claw of a hand on my arm.

"Come and see me soon," she said. "I've got something I think you should see. I haven't told anyone about it, certainly not Jens who'd want it for his museum, but since you're writing a book about the Pompineaus it's only fair to let you see it."

"Thank you, Miss Gussie, I'll be glad to."

On the way downstairs Mr. Andersen gave me the key to the padlock.

"I'll have a new lock on the door as soon as possible. In the meantime you'll probably want to examine the room more closely."

He started to say something more but apparently changed his mind. Then, his blue eyes troubled, he said quickly, "Please be careful, Miss Alix. There's a feel of anger in this house. I don't like it—I don't like it at all."

Anger. Yes, the house was filled with it. Anger against me, the intruder, whose lineage made me irrevocably an enemy and a target for vengeance. That blow between my shoulders on the tower steps had not been my imagination.

I could feel the warmth of my body leave me. I shivered with a sudden chill that was as shocking as a plunge into icy water.

This, then, was fear, the kind of fear that had haunted my father to the day he died.

I bit down hard on my lip to keep it from trembling. Now, if ever, was the time to leave this house, to escape from the hatred that exuded from the very walls, to put all thought of the Pompineaus out of my mind forever. Now, before it was too late.

To run, then, like a coward? To flee from Claire who

had welcomed my coming; who in some way I felt but could not understand, wanted me to stay?

I shook my head. My lips were like cardboard but I managed a stiff smile.

"I am not afraid," I lied.

I decided to get my promised visit to Miss Gussie out of the way before settling down in earnest to a study of the material Mr. Andersen had put at my disposal, so a few days later I went over to St. Sebastian. The water of the harbor was smooth as a mirror except where it was broken by the frothy wake of some small boat skimming over the surface. As we neared the waterfront, Darwin called my attention to a number of small sloops swaying on their moorings at the sea wall. On the concrete pavement in front of them a swarm of black men and women were busily engaged in sorting into separate piles a colorful cargo of fruit and vegetables.

"F'um Tortola," he explained. "Bring plantains an' co'ke'nuts." He raised his arm, tilted his head back and pretended to drink thirstily. "Co'ke'nut water plenty good," he grinned and wiped his mouth on his arm.

The sun was hot and the air smelled faintly of fish. I was glad to leave the boat and the noisy waterfront behind me and make my way to the main street. To my right I could see high above the street, the pink and white hotel.

"The house belonged originally to a Danish merchant named Jensen," Miss Gussie told me in the dim, deserted combination dining room and bar where we sat and sipped the cold pink planters' punch she mixed for us. "There was a son, Knud, who was aide to the governor. He lived in St. Croix but spent some time now and then in this house. I'll show you his room later."

Her little blue eyes regarded me knowingly over her glass.

"How can you be sure it was his room after so many years?"

She cocked her head on one side like a parrot. "You'll see! I'll show you."

"Well," she went on, "feeling was running high among the slaves on St. Croix because the governor was largely responsible for an ordinance from Denmark postponing their freedom. Knud Jensen came over from St. Croix, probably to size up the situation here. It was known that he and Claire had met at Claire's birthday ball and that they obviously had been attracted to each other, yet when he disappeared mysteriously at about the same time that Claire did, no one seems to have connected the two events."

"I suppose they thought he'd been killed by the slaves."

Miss Gussie nodded. "And his body thrown into the sea. Well, the Jensens went back to Denmark and the house was sold. It changed hands a good many times and was in pretty bad condition when I bought it. My last husband had just decamped with a rich-bitch tourist and I needed something to occupy my mind so I practically tore the house apart fixing it up. Have another drink? No? Come along, then, and I'll show you how I know a certain room was Knud's."

We went out to the patio and climbed the worn, stone steps to the floor above. I followed Miss Gussie along the gallery to a room at the front of the house. She opened the jalousied door with a key she fished from her capacious pocket.

"This is my room," she said. "Come on in."

It was a large, square room with two windows at the front facing the harbor and two at the side overlooking the small, brick-paved patio of a house next door. Miss Gussie went to one of the front windows and motioned for me to follow.

"Look," she said, pointing a long, red fingernail at some letters carved into the wood of a jalousied shutter.

I leaned closer. The letters were small and neat and had been carved deeply.

"C. P." I read aloud.

Miss Gussie lifted her finger from the carving and pointed dramatically at the white house on the cliff at Mon Domaine.

"I believe that Knud Jensen must have stood here often looking at the house Claire lived in. I think he was in love with her and carved her initials here on the shutter."

"It's a romantic idea and could be true," I said. "Did such a romance really exist?"

"Really exist?" she snorted. "Of course it did. Oh,

63

there's nothing in the records but I've got proof. Here, let me show you."

She went to a mahogany highboy that stood between the other two windows and pulled out one of the drawers.

"Came with the house," she said. "It had been painted green at one time and was in very bad condition but I could see it was a good piece. I decided to have it redone but first I gave it a good scrubbing. Back in the corner of this drawer was a wide crack and wedged into it I found—this!"

She took something from the drawer and held it out to me.

It was a ring, a small one with six stones of different colors in a gold setting.

"What an odd selection of stones," I said turning the ring around in my fingers.

"Name them."

I was surprised but did what she asked.

"The first one's coral and this dark blue one is lapis lazuli, isn't it? The next one's an amethyst. Then there's a cameo—I've never seen such a small one. The last two are a ruby and an emerald. Why in the world would anyone choose such an odd combination?"

"Try spelling their initials."

"C," I began. "L,A—why, it's going to spell Claire, isn't it? Oh no, the next one is C for cameo."

"Go on," said Miss Gussie.

"R and E. They don't spell anything."

"That's what I thought at first. Take another look at the cameo—is the figure raised from the background?"

"No, it's carved into the stone. Of course! It's an intaglio. The stones do spell Claire."

"You see?" Miss Gussie's shrewd little eyes were bright with triumph.

"I believe Knud had this ring made and never got a chance to give it to her. Jacques would certainly have opposed any romance between the daughter he adored and the aide to the governor he hated."

"If Jacques hated the governor so much why did he invite him to the ball?"

"Protocol. The Danes were strong for it. Even the wealthy slave owners who hated the governor had to attend."

I turned the little ring over in my fingers. "Poor Claire," I sighed. "What do you suppose happened to the two young lovers?"

"Who knows? Maybe Jacques caught them and in a fit of rage killed them both. Maybe Knud tried to smuggle her over to St. Croix and they were caught and killed by rebel slaves. All we know is that Jacques could never bear to enter her room or hear her name spoken."

I held out the ring but Miss Gussie wouldn't take it.

"No," she said. "I want you to have it. You're young, like Claire. You even look a little bit like the way she's said to have looked. Wear it for her."

I never did.

That night when I went to bed I laid the ring on my dresser. The next morning it was still there but twisted out of shape as if it had been crushed in an iron grip.

I had locked the door before turning out the light the night before. I knew I had, because before tucking the mosquito net under the mattress I had gone back to the door and made sure it was properly secured.

Now, my nerves quivering and my mind sick with apprehension, I grasped the door knob. It turned in my hand but the door did not budge. The key was still in the lock.

Someone who had no need of keys had been in my room while I slept.

I thought of Claire but dismissed the thought at once. It was no friendly spirit that had crushed the ring into a shapeless mass.

Where had she been when my room was entered? Was she powerless against the evil that still existed in the chateau?

Chapter 6

In view of the events of the previous night it seemed to me that the chateau must be a house divided against itself, for clearly, the force that had thrown me down the tower stairs was in violent opposition to me, while the gentle presence that had walked beside me to my room was definitely friendly. It was the latter's hand, I was sure, that had put the flashlight and slipper on my dresser. Although I had seen the spectral face of Brandish suffused with anger and "heard" his voice almost suffocated with rage, I did not believe that it was he who had laid in wait for me in the observatory. Indeed I had thought him more pathetic than menacing with his straggling locks, unshaven face and terror-filled eyes fixed on the weapon descending with deadly accuracy upon his old, gray head. I could imagine him resenting me as an intruder in the ancestral home of the Pompineaus, but not to the extent of removing me by murder. "Over my dead body," he had said to the visitor who had come by night, and over his dead body I had gained access to his home and to the secrets of his wasted life. Brandish had been a drunkard, not a criminal, a weak descendant of cruel, rapacious forbears, a recluse who had sought oblivion in the bottle. Which, then, of the other ghostly Pompineaus, I wondered, had reason to wish me dead?

I had chosen the library as the room in which I could best work without fear of interruption, and it was there that I went this morning after breakfast. I had no wish to sit at the table where Brandish had been killed; instead, I established myself at the opposite side of the room with two handsome card tables pushed together as a desk and a chess table inlaid with mother-of-pearl at my side to hold the reference material Jens Andersen had given me. Before long I heard the crunch of the jeep's wheels on the driveway and the hearty "Hallo!" that always heralded Jens' arrival, followed by Abby's invariably cheerful "Good morning" and smiled at the obvious pleasure in their voices. Then, opening the first of a series of folders labelled in Jens' beautiful printing, I settled down to a study of what, although still strange to me, was a record of my own family background.

The account of the sinking of Jean Pompineau's pirate ship in the harbor of St. Sebastian, his ensuing sponsorship by the governor, and the gift of land on the peninsula then known as Eye of the Needle as a site for his magnificent chateau was set forth in a treatise by an indignant clergyman of the day under the title "The Shame of Piracy Abetted by Corruption in High Places." On the cover was a woodcut of a swaggering giant with ferocious eyes and a luxuriant black beard reaching to the buckle of a wide belt hung with a brace of pistols. The further exploits of my infamous ancestor and his equally infamous descendants might better have been left unrecorded, for a nastier record of evil doing is beyond imagination.

In a letter written in 1831 by a society lady to her husband, a government official temporarily absent from the island, I came across the first reference to hidden treasure.

"It was exceedingly kind of you to permit me to attend the soirée at the chateau without your presence as my escort. Your uncle performed that service with admirable savoir faire considering his aversion to social affairs where he is required to make small talk.

"Mere words do not suffice to describe the splendors within the chateau—my head swims when I endeavor to recall the wonders that I saw—the furniture made of rare woods and covered in rich brocade, the silk and satin draperies, the oriental rugs, the ornaments of gold and silver and porcelain. What opulence, what elegance! I suspect the existence of a secret room filled with chests overflowing with jewels and coins of gold and silver, for without such treasure how could the Pompineaus have continued for so many years to live in a splendor rivalling that of royal potentates?"

I laid the letter on the table before me and closing my eyes tried to visualize the melancholy room in which I sat as it must have appeared to the eyes of the lady who lacked words to describe it.

Hidden treasure? It was a romantic idea and I was all for believing it. Somewhere, perhaps, in the old, dusty ledgers at my elbow there might be a clue to its hiding place.

I had asked for a tray to be brought to me at lunch time but, engrossed in my work, had scarcely noticed when it was set down beside me. Now, long past noon, I looked with distaste at the limp lettuce, the half-dissolved mold of gelatin, the glass of pale, tepid tea and worst of all, the ball of pink, flaked fish topped with oily mayonnaise disintegrating upon the lettuce.

Surely Delfina was aware of my aversion for canned salmon—she'd seen me refuse it before—so what reason could she have for serving it other than to annoy me? And why, for heaven's sake, should she want to do that? Could she possibly have an inkling of my real identity and be fearful for her future security in my employ? But that was nonsense, of course. No one except Abby knew that I was a Pompineau and wild horses couldn't drag that information from her without my consent.

Shrugging it off as unimportant, I began again to think about the possibility of hidden treasure. If Brandish had survived the fatal attack on his life, would he have revealed the presence of a secret room in the chateau to the chosen legatees of his estate rather than risk its discovery by some imposter or even by a legal descendant of the family like myself? Why had there been no mention of it in his will if, as I wanted to believe, it really existed? What manner of man had my cousin Brandy really been? According to Mr. Andersen he had lived for many years on the family sugar plantation on St. Croix and his life there had been far from exemplary. Why, then, in his later years, had he shut himself up in the chateau and refused to see anyone? What had he meant by "over my dead body"? Over my dead body—what?

Thinking about him brought a vivid memory to mind of the vision I had seen of his death. I shuddered and found myself resisting a compulsion to look at the writing table, dreading a repetition of the murder scene, yet in spite of my resolution I was overcome by a force stronger than my will to resist it that drew my eyes to the fatal spot. I may have screamed—I probably did—but no sound passed my lips and I could not have moved a muscle if my life had depended on it.

As before, two figures faced each other across the table on which there was now a lighted lamp, a map spread open and weighed down, a long-barreled pistol, a crystal decanter three-quarters full of ruby-colored wine and two glasses holding a few drops of the liquid.

As I watched, one of the men reached for the decanter, removed the stopper and refilled the glasses. He was broad and powerfully built and his florid, heavy-jowled face was crowned with a curling mop of auburn hair. The eyes could have been blue or green but were sunk so deep into the flesh surrounding them that the color was indistinguishable. His mouth was small and pursy, and as he set down his glass he patted his lips with a forefinger on which he wore a large set with a glowing ruby. His suit was made of white silk and the frills on his shirt were edged with lace.

No sound broke the absolute silence in the room, but suddenly I was conscious of a slight movement in the foyer. Turning my head I saw two figures in the doorway, a blond-haired young man in a white uniform with gold epaulettes, and Claire, in a pink lace gown with small silk rosebuds among the flounces of her wide, hooped skirt. She raised her hand and touched the man's arm as if to restrain him from entering the room, but he shook his head and put a finger to his lips for silence. I had no idea how long they had been standing there, but by the expression on their faces they would seem to have heard something that had shocked and angered them.

The men at the table raised their wine glasses to each other. The heavier and elder of the two whom I presumed to be the host, shaped his small mouth in an unpleasant smile. The almost eerie silence in the room remained unbroken, yet when his lips moved in speech I heard each word distinctly.

"To tomorrow," he said. "May your aim be perfect and your trigger finger steady."

"I'll not fail you," replied the other.

"Make sure that you don't." He raised his brimming glass to his lips and a few drops fell on the white suit, staining it like blood and the ruby on his finger gleamed red in the lamplight. The man in the white uniform crossed the room swiftly. Raising his arm, he pointed his finger dramatically at the man in the silk suit. His words snapped like the crack of a whiplash. "Jacques Pompineau, in the name of His Majesty the King, I denounce you as the instigator of a plot to assassinate the Governor. You and your accomplice will be taken into custody and charged with treason."

Jacques Pompineau drained his glass and set it on the table. The ruddy color had left his face but the hand on his glass was steady.

"Poppycock!" he sneered. "Who's to sustain your word against mine?"

"I will," said Claire.

She advanced into the room passing so close to my chair that her swaying, ruffled skirt brushed against my knee. She walked to her father and tilting her head back so far that her auburn hair fell almost to her waist, stared up into his arrogant face.

"I will bear witness to your perfidy," she said. "I will repeat every word of your foul plot against a good and noble man whom you hate because he pities the slaves you treat worse than your horses and dogs. I repudiate you forever as a murderer, in intent, if not by act."

He put out a hand to touch her, but she shrank away from him.

"Claire," he begged. "I am your father. I love you better than anything in the world. How can you threaten to betray me? What do you know of politics? My child, you do not know what you are saying."

"I know very well what I am saying. I came to this room tonight with the man I love to ask you one more time for your consent to our marriage. I thought you were alone. I could never have believed that you would permit anyone like Cash Hawks to enter this house, who's nothing but a cheap politician greedy for money and position. And you, my father, have hired him to do murder for you! Oh, yes, I listened, and every word I heard branded you a criminal. I will not remain under this roof with you any longer. Knud shall take me to his mother and tomorrow at first light, we will go together to the Governor."

Jacques turned to the young man who stood rigid, his arms at his sides, his hands clenched into fists.

"Do not act hastily," he said. "Let us be sensible and come to an agreement. I guarantee that the Governor shall come to no bodily harm through me on the morrow or at any time in the future. In return for your silence I will grant permission for your marriage to my daughter. She shall have a fortune as her dowry. Come, give me your hand on it."

Knud raised his fist and struck the proffered hand with such force that Jacques staggered and clutched at the table for support.

"I'll see you hang first!"

As the last words left his lips Knud Jensen clutched his breast, stood rigid for a long moment and then sagged to the floor.

Cash Hawks slowly lowered the pistol. I had heard no sound but I now saw the wisp of smoke that drifted from the barrel of the deadly weapon.

Claire screamed as Knud's body struck the floor. Then, throwing herself on her knees beside him, she put her arm under his head and struggled to raise it from the floor and into her arms.

"My love, my love," she moaned. "Look at me, speak to me. I won't let you die, my darling."

Her body curved over him like a flower broken on its stem. Jacques stared down at her, his face ashen with fear.

"My God, Cash, what have you done?" he gasped.

The other shrugged. "Saved you from the gallows, I'd say. Or will, in a minute."

He raised the gun, cocked it and took careful aim at a spot between Claire's white shoulders.

"We're lost if she lives to talk!" He flung the words at Jacques without taking his eyes from the place at which he was aiming.

"No!" screamed Jacques, "Not at your filthy hands!"

He lunged for the cumbersome revolver, seized it and pointed it toward the ceiling. The small, wiry figure of Cash Hawks leaped into the air, fastened his hands on Jacques' wrist, bore it down and wrenched it so that the gun was in line with Claire's shoulders.

"Shoot!" he panted.

A tell-tale wisp of smoke trailed from the muzzle as the gun fell from Jacques' hand to the floor and seemed to spread until I was surrounded by a gray mist.

I do not know how long I sat in that room of horror where three times I had witnessed cold-blooded murder. When I became aware of my surroundings and could move my stiffened muscles I struggled to my feet and stood swaying, gripping the card table for support.

The room was empty. The table near the French window was bare except for a crystal bowl of pink hibiscus and a trailing vine of coralita—which I, myself, had placed there when I entered the room after breakfast.

I could not bear to remain another instant in that fateful library: even if my legs would not support me and I had to crawl on my hands and knees I knew that I must escape. I took a step. Something gave under my foot, something small and soft. Quickly I withdrew my foot and stooping, took the small object in my fingers. Numb with shock I stared at it with utter disbelief, a silk rosebud with a shred of pink lace clinging to it.

If ever I were to be asked whether I actually felt the substance of the tiny object under my foot or sensed the tangible reality of silk and lace with my fingertips, I could not swear to the truth of it for even as I gazed in fascinated wonder, the fragmentary evidence of Claire's presence faded into nothingness before my eyes.

Chapter 7

The lobby of the Majestic Hotel where I'd been invited to meet Jon for lunch was vast, high-ceilinged, and deliciously cool. A flight of broad carpeted steps leading up to it from the street level presented over its wide mahogany handrail an unobstructed view of the interior of a gift shop below.

Passing from the hot, noisy street crowded with tourists into the quiet, fan-cooled, old-fashioned splendor of the lobby was like taking a step backward in time to an age of leisure and gracious living.

Just as I entered, the siren on the nearby fort emitted a scream so earsplitting that I came to a shocked standstill. A group of tourists I'd seen debarking from a cruise ship earlier that morning halted suddenly in their passage to the bar at the far end of the room. As the last wail died away one of the men exclaimed, "By God, the whole town must be on fire! We'd better get back to the ship."

The noise had been shattering and I turned with relief as I heard Jon's voice behind me.

"Infernal racket, wasn't it?" he asked.

"What on earth is it? A jail break, a hurricane warning or what?"

"Nothing so exciting—just our West Indian custom of

announcing the noon hour. To calm your nerves I suggest a banana daiquiri. But first I'd like you to see something interesting." He gestured to the wall at our left which was hung with paintings. "All by local artists. One picture, in particular, I think you'll like."

We stopped in front of a large canvas framed in a band of unpolished, silvery metal: In the foreground a square, gray house with a wide porch spanning its width, two broad, shallow steps leading up to it from a hibiscus-bordered driveway; in the background some low buildings sprawling around a larger one of two stories with a tall brick chimney—at a little distance one of the old, round stone sugar mills, a few of which still stand in ruins on St. Sebastian, and, surrounding it, a field of sugar cane in full, silvery-mauve bloom.

"Estate Le Sucrier on St. Croix," said Jon. "It belonged to the Pompineaus until ten years ago when Brandish sold it to Miles Kitteredge, the movie star who wanted to retire there and breed race horses."

"Miles Kitteredge? He was killed in a plane crash, wasn't he? I remember how the girls at school wept and carried on when the news came out."

"Yes, that was right after he bought Le Sucrier. His son Mark inherited the Kitteredge fortune and turned the plantation into an exclusive resort with a private golf course that attracts professionals. He runs the resort like a sugar plantation on a miniature scale, grows a little cane and grinds it in the mill—that building with the chimney—as an added attraction for the guests. Every year he gives a ball in the old plantation style—this year it's to be a costume affair, reproducing Claire's birthday ball in eighteen forty-eight."

"Miles Kitteredge had two sons, hadn't he?"

"That's right. The younger one, Jerry, was killed in an auto accident about eight years ago. Well, now that you've seen the Pompineau Sugar Bowl, how about that banana daiquiri?"

We crossed the lobby to a gallery overlooking a public garden and the waterfront. Beyond lay the bright blue water of the harbor and the darker blue of the open sea.

Jon stood for a moment running his eyes over the many square tables on the gallery, each with its complement of rattan chairs, most of which were already occupied. A large, round table dominated the open-air dining room. Seated around it were several men and one woman engaged in noisy conversation frequently interrupted by bursts of laughter. As they caught sight of us they waved at Jon and gave me the frankly curious stare old-timers everywhere reserve for a newcomer. I was pleased by the little spark of admiration that appeared in the eyes of the men but definitely not in those of the woman. At the airport where I had previously seen her I had been impressed by her exquisite coloring and the exceptional beauty of her eyes. Now, however, a heavy application of make-up made her look brazen, and her eyes, as she stared at me were as hard and cold as blue marbles.

When we had found a table and ordered our drinks, Jon mentioned the group at the round table.

"The men are regulars, here every day rain or shine, except the fellow in the white turtleneck—I've never seen him before."

I glanced casually at the dark-haired, olive-skinned man in the white sweater.

"Almost too good looking, isn't he?" I commented. "Looks as if he'd stepped from the pages of *Gentlemen's Quarterly*. Who's the girl?"

Jon's pleasant face clouded. "She's Mrs. Mark Kitteredge," he said.

"You don't like her, do you?"

He shook his head. "I know her too well to like anything about her. Besides, Mark is my friend; I don't like to see him hurt."

So the man at the airport, with the thin, white scar on his cheek and the funny little cowlick in his hair was Mark Kitteredge, this woman's husband and the father of the little red-headed boy!

"What's he like?—her husband, I mean."

"Mark? He's a great guy—they don't come any better."

I was absurdly pleased, as if the compliment had been paid to an intimate friend instead of a complete stranger. My one fleeting glimpse into Mark's mind had been like a preview of light-hearted adventure; an exciting prospect for one whose life had hitherto been as uneventful as mine.

We were enjoying our drinks when a confusion of voices and a loud scraping of chairs on the tiled floor drew my attention again to the round table. Linda Kitteredge and the handsome stranger were leaving and the others were signing their lunch checks and digging into their pockets for change. One of them left the group and came over to our table, a big, heavy-set man with close-cut brown hair, shrewd, caramel-colored eyes under heavy brows, full lips and a square chin cleft by a deep dimple. He laid a large well-manicured hand on Jon's shoulder and beamed at me over his head.

"I'm Tom Turner," he said. His voice was like honey, an actor's voice.

"And this is Miss Alix Bonney," said Jon, smiling to me. "Miss Bonney is on the island as a guest of the historical society. Sit down, Tom."

"Thanks, but I've only got a minute. I'm due back in Court at two o'clock and have to pick up some papers at the office first. Thought you'd like to hear the latest. See that fellow who left with Linda? His name is Darcy, André Darcy, and he says he's the great-grandson of Louis Pompineau."

"Good Lord!" Jon gave a low whistle of astonishment. "You mean he's here to claim the estate?"

"If he can. Brandy was no fool; I drew the will, you know. He left a sixty-four dollar question in a sealed envelope as a final test for any claimant. If Darcy can answer it he's in."

"But that's impossible!" My voice shook with indignation.

Both men looked startled by my vehemence.

"On the contrary, Miss Bonney." Tom Turner leveled a finger at me to emphasize his point. "It is quite possible that Louis Pompineau settled in France, married and raised a family under the assumed name of Darcy."

"True," said Jon, "but can this fellow prove it?"

"Says he can. Described the Le Sucrier as it was in Louis' time. Linda's taking him over there to stay. Well I'd better be off. Nice meeting you, Miss Bonney. See you around, Jon."

I took a cigarette from my case on the table. Jon leaned forward with his lighter.

"Now, Miss Georgia Bonney," he said looking me straight in the eye, "What was all that about?"

"What was all what about?"

"All that indignation, high color and flashing eyes. What makes you so sure Darcy is a phoney?"

"I didn't say that."

"You didn't need to. Look, sugar, if you have reason to believe this fellow is an imposter, and I think you believe just that, you owe it to the people of St. Sebastian to expose him as such. The chateau as a tourist attraction would be an added source of income to the island. Besides, it belongs to them as a part of their history. No one has a right to deprive them of it unless he has a valid claim and I think you're sure he hasn't."

He sat back and waited for me to speak. I tried to arrange my thoughts in orderly sequence. First, I liked Jon. Although publicity was his business I felt sure I could trust him with the secret of my identity. He was intelligent. He would know how to advise me to handle this unexpected situation; and finally, I could do with a lot of good advice at this point.

"All right," I said. "I do know beyond the shadow of a doubt that this André Darcy is an imposter. The proof dates back to a day when I was six years old and found a painting of the chateau in an old trunk in the attic."

The words came pouring out. My father's coldness toward me; his strange reaction to the sight of the picture in my hands, the padlocked door, his sudden death, the letter and photograph crushed down into the side of his chair; Louis' confession and my father's letter, and my determination to establish my own identity to my own satisfaction. "And," I added, "to get to the bottom of this business about the curse."

"So," said Jon when I had finished, "that makes you the rightful heir to the Pompineau estate."

I nodded. "An estate that I am not at all sure I want."

"Understood. But one that must not be allowed to fall into the hands of an imposter. I wonder who he is and where he got his information? I don't imagine there are any copies of the papers in Jens' collection. Where else could he get the inside information he's supposed to have? He must be pretty sure of himself to take such a chance on getting away with a hoax like this. By the way, who, besides me, knows about the painting?"

"Only Abby."

"Then Jens doesn't know who you are?"

"No. I'd rather he didn't. I've never met anyone before, except Abby, whose good opinion of me has mattered so much. I'm ashamed of being a Pompineau and I don't want Jens to think the less of me because of it."

"You've a mighty poor opinion of him if you think he would. What really would hurt him would be to find out that you've kept it from him."

"But if he never finds out he can't be hurt by it, can he?"

Jon snorted. "Now there's a specious argument if ever I heard one. What you're saying is that what Jens don't know can't hurt him. That's where you're wrong, Miss Georgia Bonney Pompineau. By your silence you're giving Darcy a green light in his scheme to defraud Jens and the historical society. Do you want that to happen?"

"Good heavens, no!"

"Then go to Jens now and tell him the truth about yourself. Give him the word about Darcy and put him on his guard against the fellow and his pretensions that are sure to sound plausible. Incidentally, are you learning much from your research?"

"Plenty, most of it nasty. Tell me, was there ever an attempt to assassinate the governor of the islands?"

"Yes, once, back in eighteen forty-eight, but not by a Pompineau, though Jacques might well have had a hand in it. He was one of the rich, slave-owning planters who hated the governor for his policy of freeing the slaves, and while nothing was ever proved against any of them there was plenty of talk. The governor was making a speech in the slave market, which, by the way still stands in St. Croix, when a politician by the name of Hawks shot at him but missed. When the crowd turned on him he put a bullet through his own head."

A picture flashed through my mind of the two men in the library with glasses raised to each other. I heard the threat in Jacques' voice as he said, "Make sure that you don't," and saw again the drop of red wine falling on his white suit, staining it the color of the blood-red ruby on his finger.

The horror of reliving the scene must have shown on my face for Jon gave my hand a reassuring pat.

"I shouldn't have made it so graphic," he apologized. "You look as if you've been seeing ghosts. And speaking of ghosts, do you ever get the feeling, as Jens does, of a presence of evil in the chateau?"

I hesitated. Should I tell him of the attempt on my life in the tower and of Claire's ring crushed into a shapeless mass of gold and jewels by someone or something that could enter and leave my locked room at will? If I described my visions wouldn't he be justified in classifying them as the hallucinations of a mind unbalanced by fear? Worse still, wouldn't he insist that it was too dangerous for me to remain in the chateau?

So I smiled and told a bare-faced lie. "No," I said. "If there is anything evil in the house it's keeping out of my way. Besides, I'm not afraid of the supernatural."

I was to regret the cocksureness of those words before twenty-four hours had passed.

The next morning, stooping to retrieve an earring that had rolled under the bed, I found a small wax figure dressed in a swatch of cloth that had been cut from one of my dresses. A wisp of auburn hair had been glued to the head which bristled with glass-headed pins deeply imbedded in it.

I straightened up, the doll in my hands. Instantly I gasped with pain and flung it from me. The room swam in front of my eyes and the sudden pain in my head was almost unbearable. It passed immediately but left me feeling sick and dizzy.

Somewhere, buried in my mind, was a word that stood for what was happening to me. I struggled to bring it to the surface and when it came I shrank from it fearfully.

"Obeah!" I whispered, my eyes on the little wax figure on the floor.

Someone who wished me harm was using the dread West Indian witchcraft against me.

Chapter 8

The observatory at the top of the tower was, I decided, the only place in the chateau where it would be possible to converse without danger of being overheard. The balcony outside the windows was inaccessible except from within the room since the rough stone outer walls provided no foothold, and the small platform on the roof from which the flags were raised and lowered could be reached only by a narrow ladder and a trap door at one end of the observatory. Opening into the room from a landing at the top of the spiral staircase was a heavy door with an old-fashioned latch.

I was becoming increasingly aware of Delfina's hostility and on several occasions when leaving a room had caught the flutter of her flounced skirt whisking through a nearby door. I had no doubt that it was she who had put the wax doll under my bed. Although I had burned the effigy and buried the pins in a flower bed I still suffered an occasional sharp, momentary pain in my head. The woman seemed to be everywhere. Only in the observatory behind the closed door was I safe from those burning eyes and listening ears.

I did not like the room. Even in broad daylight, with every window thrown wide, there was the sense of an alien presence, a thing without substance, a soundless vibration of the atmosphere.

We were there, Abby, Jens and I, seated in Captain's chairs that were drawn up to a large flat-topped mahogany desk on which I had put the rolled-up painting and the letter from my father.

"I suppose you're wondering why I asked you to come up here instead of to any of the other rooms," I said. "It's because I want to avoid the possibility of our being overheard."

Then turning to Jens, I said, "We know that Brandish died believing himself to be the last of his line. It is also a fact that in willing the estate to the St. Sebastian Historical Society he stipulated that a waiting-period of one year be observed, after which anyone claiming direct descendance in the Pompineau line should be given the opportunity to present proof of his claim." I paused. Jens nodded and Abby smiled, her eyes on the painting and the letter. "I have learned," I went on, "that such a person has recently arrived in San Sebastian for that purpose. I have seen him and have been told his name is André Darcy."

"Darcy?" Jens looked puzzled. "I don't recall any mention of that name in the records."

"It's a mistake, of course," said Abby. "Alix has proof."

"Proof? Of what?"

I drew a deep breath and hoped he wouldn't mind too much that I hadn't taken him into my confidence before.

"Proof," I said, "that whether I like it or not I am the great-granddaughter of Louis Pompineau."

Jens' eyebrows flew up. "Himmel! You knew this before you came to San Sebastian?"

"I had only just discovered it. I came in search of my real identity."

Jens glanced at Abby. "You say there is proof?"

I unrolled the canvas and laid it face-up on the table. "I found this in an old trunk in our attic," I said.

He bent over the painting, studying every detail, pausing now and then to put his finger on some particular spot, uttering excited commentaries in Danish, as lost in delight as a child at Christmas. I gave him time, then said, "Now look at the back."

He turned it over, scanned the first few words, and then read aloud the confession penned by the man who had chosen to call himself Louis Bonney. At the end he raised his eyes and gave me a long, searching look.

"To my descendants," he quoted with a rising reflection on the last word.

I handed him my father's letter. "The answer is here," I said.

Abby took my hand and held it while we both watched his face as he read. When he had finished he read it a second time, then folded it back into the original age-stained creases.

"Alix, how did your father die?" he asked.

I hesitated, recalling the neat signature on the letter from the historical society.

"He'd had a shock," I said slowly. "He was recovering from the flu and was still very weak."

"It was my letter, wasn't it? I am very sorry."

Abby made a little gesture of protest. "Please don't blame yourself, Jens—you couldn't have known that the picture would have any significance for him. We know now that he had lived for years in the expectation of sudden death. He had few relatives but they had all died by violence and his wife was killed by a bullet intended for him. Is it any wonder that he believed in the curse and feared it?"

Remembering, I said, "He once told me 'It is not a good thing to live with fear.' In the end it killed him."

Jens asked, "You are not afraid?"

I looked into his honest blue eyes and could not lie. "Yes, I am afraid, not of the curse, because I believe it died with Brandish, but of the evil that lives on and seems to be indestructible. The genes of thieves and murderers are in me—I wish I had never found out who I am!"

In his eyes I saw a shadow of reproof.

"You are the first of a new breed of Pompineaus, freed forever, by Brandy's death, from the threat of the curse. It's your responsibility to make your name a symbol of pride instead of shame. The past is gone. The evil will go, too."

"Some day, perhaps. But can a word, once spoken, ever be unsaid?" I paused. "Anathema Maranatha," I said, and shuddered.

Abby repeated the words. "They frighten me," she added, "and I'm not even sure what they mean."

Some of the fresh color left Jens' face. "Condemned by God," he said. " 'Let him be accursed!' Those words must have rung in Jacques' ears for the rest of his life. Do you know how he died? No? I will tell you. He hung himself, here in this room. There was no one to mourn him. His own son detested him."

I looked around the room, nervously, I must admit. Where was he hanging when they found him?

And then I saw it, set into one of the heavy wooden rafters. What its original use had been I could not guess, but there it was, an iron hook like those one sees in a butcher shop with a bloody carcass of an animal impaled upon it. It was fixed so high above the floor that Jacques would have had to stand on a chair in order to fling a rope over it, and then with the noose around his neck, kick the chair from under him and swing slowly, and more slowly, in the ghastly parody of a dance.

Jens was still speaking, "There are stories, still whispered by the natives, that Jacques' son defied the curse and swore to raze the chateau to the ground. Shortly after, when he plunged to his death from the balcony outside this room, they were quick to believe it was neither accident nor suicide but murder."

"Murder!" exclaimed Abby. "Committed by the house? What a fantastic idea!'

"Not to people who believe in witchcraft. Obeah is still practised right here on St. Sebastian. It's a very effective means of getting rid of one's enemy. Absolutely foolproof, too. One doesn't get caught, you see."

My head throbbed suddenly and violently—my hand, as I touched it to my forehead, was like ice. Why had I been so naive as to believe that Delfina's attempt to harm me would confine itself to a wax doll stuck full of pins? Even now some kind of spell might be working against me.

Abby was speaking. "I, for one, put no stock in ghost stories about this house. I have not seen or heard or felt anything to indicate that it is haunted."

"Haunted?" Jens shook his head. "Nej, it is more than that. The house is possessed. You are left in peace because you are not here to pry into its secrets. Alix feels the presence of evil as I, too, feel it. I wonder how it will receive this Darcy fellow. How much do you know about him, Alix?"

"Very little, really. I saw him last Friday when I had lunch with Jon at the Majestic. He was with a group at another table. He is about my age or a little older, good looking in a spectacular sort of way, olive complexion, dark, wavy hair worn a little long, vivid personality, talks a lot with his hands, moves as gracefully as a flamenco dancer. He was very attentive to a woman Jon said was Mrs. Kitteredge and after lunch they left together. It was a man named Tom Turner who told us that Darcy claims to be the great-grandson of Louis Pompineau."

Jens flicked his finger against my father's letter. "He'll need more than his word to disprove this!"

"Including," I said, "the right answer to a question Brandish sealed in an envelope and gave to Tom Turner."

"Ja, I know. I was present at the reading of the will."

"Of course that applies to me, too. I wish I knew whatever it is that I'm supposed to know."

"The question," said Abby thoughtfully, "has to refer to something that only a Pompineau could know. A family secret, I mean, that's been handed down from generation to generation."

Jens nodded. "The answer may even be hidden somewhere in the painting."

I pointed to the lower right hand corner of the canvas where a signature in miniscule letters had been blended into the background so skillfully as to be barely discernible.

"It is signed Bonney," I said.

"Louis?" asked Abby.

"No, just Bonney."

"There was once a woman pirate by that name," mused Jens. "She might have come here as a guest of some early Pompineau and painted the picture as a gift. However, she lived in the early seventeen hundreds, long before the hill was terraced and these steps in the picture were added. Perhaps it was Louis who did the painting after he left here and changed his name."

"I wonder why he chose that particular one," I said. "Maybe it was the nickname of a close friend."

Abby smiled. "Or of a girl he was fond of."

"No, he'd hardly have treasured a reminder of Christine after the way she jilted him. Jens, can you think of anyone mentioned in the records whose name might have been shortened to Bonney?"

He struck the flat of his hand against his forehead. "*Saa for pokker!*" he exclaimed. "Boneffet! Louise Boneffet!"

"Who was she?"

"A girl from Frenchtown in St. Croix. She was the nursemaid when the boys were young. Later she became the housekeeper."

"Boneffet," said Abby, turning the word over on her tongue. "Yes, the boys might have shortened it to Bonney. What became of her?"

"She probably went back to St. Croix. There are still people of that name living there."

"I'll go and see them," I said. "It's possible that she may have kept a journal which has been preserved."

"Ja, but it is also possible that they will not acknowledge any connection, however distant, with the chateau. It has a bad name, you know."

I pushed back my chair and stood, looking down at the painting. "On the day when I, a child, saw the chateau for the first time, I looked at it as I am looking now and saw it as a fairy-story castle where only lovely things could happen. Now I see it as it really is, a house of evil, hoarding memories of ancient crimes. I want no part of it, but I will do everything I can to keep it out of the hands of an impostor."

"Ja, that we must do. I shall begin by making it my business to meet Darcy. Does anyone, except ourselves, know of your relationship to the Pompineaus?"

"Only Jon Daley. I told him in confidence."

"He will respect it. You can trust him."

"Listen," said Abby. "If this man Darcy is really an impostor, won't he look for an excuse to get into the house, to go through the rooms and pretend to recognize things he'd say his great-grandfather had described in stories about his youth: stories that have been handed down through the years?"

Jens slapped his hand on his knee. "*Selvfølgelig!* Yes, naturally! To strengthen his claim! We must not let that happen!"

"We won't, since you are the only one who can give permission to go through the house." She laid her hand on the painting. "Mon Domaine belongs to Alix even if she

85

doesn't want it. What she does with it afterward is her business—ours is to see that she gets it."

I thanked them and told them to go on downstairs ahead of me, that I'd shut the windows myself.

The glare was terrific but when I finished with the last window and turned my back on the brilliancy of the sun-spangled sea I was startled by the almost total absence of light in the room as if thick, dark curtains had been drawn over the windows. My first thought was that even in that brief space of time a sudden tropical storm might have risen and blotted out the sun. I whirled and could not believe what I saw, for the wide expanse of water and sky was still framed in golden splendor in the glass-paned window. Myriad white-ruffled waves danced under a canopy of cloudless, blue sky. In the harbor a white gull rocked on the surface like a little boat without sails.

Terrified, I realized that something evil and threatening was in the room behind me and had to be faced. I took a deep breath, gripped my hands together to control their shaking and turned. At once I was enveloped in great whorls of gray mist trailing clammy tendrils over my face and around my throat. I clawed them away and with a tremendous effort forced my way blinding through the opaque cloud. The tendrils tightened around my throat, half strangling me. I could dimly see a face glaring at me through the fog. I knew it was Jacques and that he meant to kill me.

"Let me go!" I gasped.

I had lost all sense of direction. I was hopelessly trapped in the dense, swirling, murderous coils that crushed with the strength of steel.

The face in the fog came closer. The eyes glowed like hot coals.

Desperately I fought for breath. I opened my mouth and the scream came. I struck out at the face and screamed the terrible curse of the Pompineaus: "Anathema! Maranatha!"

The mist dissolved into nothingness. The room was flooded with sunlight. The open door was in front of me. I fled through it and down the stairs clinging to the railing to save myself from falling. On the lowest step I sank down, weak and shaken, sick with remembered fear of the formless horror that had struggled with me for my life.

My throat ached with the effort to gulp great mouthfuls of the clean, untainted air. Gradually the violent throbbing of my heart subsided and I rose shakily to my feet. I made a swift decision to say nothing to Abby and Jens about what had taken place. They would, of course, insist that I leave the chateau which I had no intention of doing until I had found where Claire's body had been hidden. Only by exposing his guilty secret could I hope to expel Jacques from the chateau.

I stooped to retrieve the canvas and the letter from the floor where I supposed they had fallen but they were not there. I searched the cream and blue rug and looked at the steps down which I had fled. I thought back to the moment when I had closed the last window in the Observatory and turned back into the fog-filled room. I relived the horror of tearing with my hands at the tendrils tightening around my throat. With my hands! *With both hands!* There had been nothing in them when I returned from the window—nothing in them when I had fled from the room. I remembered exactly how the room had looked when I had gone to close the windows—the Captain's chairs pushed back from the flat-topped table on which lay a piece of rolled-up canvas and an envelope yellow with age.

I would have to go back to that terrible room at the head of the stairs!

"No!" I cried inwardly. "No—I can't do it—I can't!"

But even as I hung back, clinging to the stair railing, my feet carried me relentlessly, step by step, to the threshold of the tower room.

I sagged against the door frame and closed my eyes against the dazzling glare reflected in the shining panes of glass. Had I really seen the amorphous cloud expunge the light from the room?

I opened my eyes. The picture and the letter were there on the table exactly as I had last seen them. Slowly I advanced into the room, each step a test of my courage, until my body touched the edge of the table. In the next second the proofs of my identity as a Pompineau were safely back in my possession. Why, I wondered, had Jacques not seized the opportunity to destroy them? Surely he knew that without them I could present no valid claim to the estate.

My eyes flew to the iron hook imbedded in the rafters.

There, hanging like a puppet clothed in white silk was Jacques, fine lace ruffles at his wrists, a blood-red ruby on his fingers.

I have no recollection of the time that elapsed between my vision of that terrible figure and the final consciousness of my presence in my own room, my body pressed against the closed door at my back, my icy hands clutching the painting and my father's letter tightly against me.

I only know that no power in the world could have swayed me then from my determination to drive Jacques from the chateau even though I had to tear the house down, brick by brick, to uncover the evidence of his heinous crime.

Chapter 9

"Boneffet?" asked Jon. "Sure, I know them—three dotty old spinsters, and a brother, Jules, a retired priest. Afraid you won't get much from the old girls, Alix, but Père Jules likes a good gossip over a glass of wine."

The sun, an incandescent crimson sphere, had just completed its spectacular evening plunge into the Caribbean: The ruby light that marked its passing was reflected on the glass top of the cocktail table and added a rosy luster to the crystal pitcher and tall glasses standing on it. It had been Abby's idea to utilize the broad, topmost landing of the terrace steps as a deck with awning and cushioned chairs where one could enjoy a pre-dinner drink and watch the nightly drama of sunset and the shy debut of the first evening stars. Also, from that viewpoint Abby and I could watch the progress of our launch from the waterfront at St. Sebastian to the landing stage at the foot of the steps, Darwin at the wheel and Jens, sometimes accompanied by other friends, arriving for his customary evening visit.

Jon leaned over, cut a wedge from the round of wine-flavored cheese on the table and helped himself to crackers. Jens, stirring the pitcher of rum punch said, "He must be getting on in years. Still a great talker, is he?"

"Whenever he can get anyone to listen. I oblige occasionally when I'm over in St. Croix."

"Then," commented Abby reasonably, "wouldn't he be more apt to talk freely to you than to a stranger like Alix?"

Jon grinned. "Don't you believe it! Père Jules has an eye for a pretty girl which Alix is and I'm not. She's also a good listener—he'll talk her ear off."

"Why not come with me?" I asked. "Two good listeners are better than one."

"Thanks, I'd like to. We can go over on an early Goose, spend a couple of hours with Père Jules and have lunch at Le Sucrier. If Miles isn't there I can show you around. When would you like to go, Miss Georgia?"

"As soon as possible. Tomorrow?"

"Why not? There's a nine-thirty flight. Darwin can run you over and I'll meet you on the waterfront."

The Goose, like its feathered prototype, follows an exhilarating pattern of take-off and flight: first a passive floating on the surface of the water gently rocked by the waves of passing craft, then a swift skimming over the surface propelled, in its natural state, by flailing wings and the thrust of strong, webbed feet and, in its metal counterpart by roaring, man-controlled power. Finally there is the triumphant rise from the water to become air-borne.

In the space of a scant half-hour of flight the memory of St. Sebastian with its steep hills and noisy, crowded streets receded into a sort of limbo in my mind, worlds removed from the charming, arcaded sidewalks of St. Croix and the level fields where sugar cane once grew higher than a man's head, and natives, their black skins glistening with sweat, swung their machetes from the "Can-see" of dawn to the "Can't-see" of dusk.

It was pleasant to sit in the courtyard of a small hotel and sip a fruit punch while Jon went to rent a car and buy a bottle of sweet wine for Père Jules. If I had not been so anxious to question the old priest I would have been tempted to suggest a leisurely walk through the quaint, old-world streets of the town and a visit to some of the intriguing little shops fronting the arcade. However, once in the car I wished only to reach our destination as quickly as possible. As we drove along the wide tree-bordered road, Jon pointed out old estates that had flourished in the days when sugar was king, and great houses, now sadly in need of repair, that had stood in proud dignity, their music-filled ballrooms gleaming in the light of a hundred candles, their mirrored walls reflecting the silks and jewels of richly attired guests.

"There's the parish church," said Jon and pointed to a white steeple showing among the leaves. "We turn off there. The Boneffet place is about a mile beyond."

A narrow dirt road, straight as a yardstick, ran through thickets of lime and guava. After a while it emerged into a settlement of small houses, each with a plot of ground devoted to flowers and vegetables. A white picket fence set one of the houses apart from the others. Within the enclosure, bending over flowerbeds, were three elderly women in starched white cotton smocks sprigged in lavender. Like a trio of flustered hens they clucked over Jon and darted sidewise glances at me from their small, glittery black eyes. One of them took the bottle presented by Jon and the others patted their hands together like children. All three then scurried into the house, chattering about glasses and sweet biscuits.

We found Père Jules napping in the shade of a mango tree at the rear of the house. A large white handkerchief covered his face, rising and falling evenly with his breathing except when an occasional snort disturbed the rhythm. His spotless white cassock was hiked halfway to his knees and his feet—enclosed in scuffed, open sandals—rested, crossed at the ankles, on an inverted bushel basket. He awoke quickly and welcomed us effusively but in spite of his willingness to talk about the chateau and its former inhabitants, he could tell us little that we did not already know.

"Louise Boneffet was engaged as a nursemaid, promoted to governess and when the children were grown, retained as housekeeper. After the quarrel between the brothers she returned to St. Croix. When she was an old woman she died and was buried in the graveyard of the Parish Church. There, mes amies, you have *la histoire* of Louise Boneffet. *Requiescat in pace!*" He made a hasty sign of the cross and drank off the wine in his glass.

I was disappointed, but accepted the fact that I had set my hopes too high. "It's sad," I said, "that a whole lifetime can be contained in a handful of words: she lived, she died, she was buried. Nothing to tell us what she looked like, whether her nature was gay or serious; whether she loved or was lovable."

Père Jules wagged a finger at me. "Au contraire," he said. "She was plain. All the Boneffets are plain—regardez—moi! You have also seen my sisters. She was of a great plainness but she was happy. She laughed, she made fun. And she loved, especially, I think, the boy, Louis."

Jon raised a skeptical eyebrow. "How come you're so sure, Père Jules? You're guessing, aren't you?"

"No, my son, I do not guess. Wait, I will tell you. Many years ago when I am a boy, I have a desire to become an artist. I cover every scrap of paper I find with my poor drawings, and one day, looking for more paper I venture into a storeroom which because it is dark and, I think, mysterious, I never before have enter. So I walk on my toes with my heart in my mouth and I find on a shelf a leather book so old that it fall apart in my hands. There are many pages, big ones. So I take the book and I find it contains pen and ink drawings. One I like very much, a young servant girl with three boys. The girl is not pretty but she have a happy face. She also have the big nose of the Boneffets."

"How I would love to have seen that book!" I exclaimed. "What became of it, Father?"

"I hid it. I did not have the courage to confess that I steal it from the storeroom." He chuckled. "I still have it. I will fetch it if you like."

He hurried away to the house. Watching him, I said, "What absolutely marvelous luck, Jon! She is Bonney, of course, and one of the boys is my great-grandfather, Louis."

A few minutes later a screen door slammed and the old priest came back, a large, manila envelope under his arm. From it he carefully extracted some sheets of drawing paper and handed the top one to me.

"Viola! Elle-même!"

The sketch was charming, picturing a girl in a high-necked, long-sleeved dress of severe cut. She was seated in a garden chair, an open book in her hands, two handsome little boys leaning over her shoulders and a third sitting at her feet, looking up at her so that the back of his head but not his face was visible. Beneath the sketch, in thin, spidery letters was written "Jacques, Louis, Bozo et moi, Bonney."

It was true, as Père Jules had said, Louise Boneffet had been plain. She had also been honest, for she had made no effort to minimize the size of her large nose or to soften the line of her square chin. Plain she had been but not drab, for her large, long-lashed eyes held the promise of ready laughter.

The boy Jacques had the look of a pirate about him—it was there in the black, unruly hair, the arrogance of posture, the bold, appraising shrewdness of ink-black eyes, the suggestion of cruelty in the thin-lipped mouth.

Comparing the two boys who were leaning over her shoulders, it was easy for me to see why Louise had especially loved the younger boy Louis with his chubby cheeks, eyes crinkled with laughter, lips curved in a merry smile and a delightful dimple in his little round chin. I could feel Jon's eyes on me and looked up. Smiling, he raised his hand and touched a finger to my chin. I smiled back and nodded. It was a nice feeling that something of that happy little boy, even so insignificant a thing as a dimpled chin, lived on in me, a visible link between us.

Père Jules had been riffling through the sheaf of sketches and now held one up for us to see.

"Ah, this one I like!" he chortled. "This one I *feel*."

With clever strokes of her pen, Louise had transferred to paper the misery and humiliation of one small boy, the angry defiance of another, and the fearsome wrath of an apoplectic old gentleman with a switch in his hand. Jacques, scowling fiercely, faced the old man, his arms at his sides, his hands clenched into fists. Beside him, Louis, fighting tears, rubbed a small bottom that obviously smarted. Under the picture Louise had written, "It is not funny to put a frog in the tobacco pouch of one's grandfather."

One of the drawings fell to the ground. Jon picked it up, studied it for a minute and then gave it to me.

"I say, Alix, look at this one. You can almost hear the noise on the waterfront and smell the fish being sold from that boat. Look, here are the boys, all three of them, buying bananas from an old crone probably over from Tortola."

Of the three boys it was the slave boy who caught and held my interest. Standing on tiptoe, one arm raised, his fingers plucking a mango off a shelf at the old woman's back, grace in every line of his body, he was a figure to delight the eye of an artist. Even I, who have no talent for art, recognized the extraordinary skill with which Louise had captured the sparkling personality of the boy; the cocky turn of his head over his shoulder; the eyes, full of mischief, fixed on the unwary fruit seller; the laughing mouth with teeth glistening white in the dark skin of his face. The picture had a strange fascination for me. I had a feeling that there was something there, something I ought to see but didn't.

I heard an exclamation of surprise and, looking up, saw Jon pointing excitedly at one of the sketches in the priest's hands.

"That's it! Exactly the same as the painting! They're identical even to the minute signature in the corner!"

Père Jules looked at him quizzically. "You have seen it before? How can that be? It has been in my possession since before you are born. It is a mistake that you make, mon cher Jean."

"We've both seen it, Father," I said. "Not this sketch, but a painting exactly like it and signed in the same way. That's why we came to see you. We thought the painting might have been done by Louise Boneffet because it was signed Bonney and we knew she had lived in the chateau. It's really very important to us."

"Then, perhaps, you will like to keep the sketch? I give it to you with pleasure."

I kissed the dear old man on the cheek, which made him blush, and when Jon teased him about it he laughed so heartily that he spilled some of the wine he was pouring into my glass.

He walked with us to the gate. The three sisters came out of the house and stood on the doorstep fluttering their hands as we left.

I had every reason to feel light-hearted; I had enjoyed my visit; I had been enchanted with Père Jules and the three old sisters in their lilac-sprigged smocks; I had seen the face of my great-grandfather, painted in his childhood by someone who loved him; I had been given a sketch made by the no-longer mysterious Bonney. I should have been happy.

I suppose that everyone at sometime or another has experienced the frustration of trying to recall a dream of which nothing remains but an impression of something tremendously important that urgently needs to be remembered. I had felt it when I looked at the picture of the slave boy, in the devil-may-care recklessness of his pose, the lithe gracefulness of his body, the hands—what was it about the hands? I had seen them before. I had seen that body. I had seen that face. But when? And where?

Chapter 10

I glanced at my watch as we turned in between the stone pillars that marked the entrance to Le Sucrier. Somewhere far ahead, a bell shattered the peaceful noonday silence with brazen clamor.

"A relic of slave days," said Jon. "Mark still uses it to call the workers from the fields although there are only a handful now compared to the numbers employed in the old days. Mark's few acres of cane are more of a stage setting than anything else but they preserve a tradition and produce enough sugar to pay for their upkeep."

As we approached the square gray house visible at the end of the long road, my heart beat faster and I realized that I was gripping my hands tightly together in my lap. What was it going to be like to meet Mark Kitteredge? Would I hear his thoughts again as I had heard them at the airport? Would I feel the same attraction that had made me turn my head for another look at the proud, suntanned face with the jagged white hairline of scar on one cheek? I didn't want to read his thoughts—or anyone else's for that matter.

"I hope to God Linda isn't here," said Jon. "The hardest thing I have to do is be decent to her."

"What's so bad about her?"

"Everything. She's been a wild one ever since she started growing up. Boy-crazy, speed-crazy, thrill-crazy, man-crazy, married or single made no difference. Anything for a kick."

"But how did she get away with it? Didn't her parents try to stop her?"

"Her mother died when Linda was a baby. Her father was a judge, and about the most respected man in the islands. Stern as hell. Linda knew damn well no one would dare put him wise. She had the cops eating out of her hand—most of them are natives and scared to death of the judge. One thing I'll never understand is how Mark could fall for her, especially after the way she'd led his kid brother on and got him running with her fast crowd. Mark tried to break it up but Jerry wouldn't listen. What really gets me is that it wasn't more than a month after his brother's funeral that Mark married her and took her on a world cruise. She's no prize, believe me." He glanced sideways at me and laughed. "Lord, Miss Georgia Bonney, I run off at the mouth worse than Père Jules—it must be catching. Well, here we are."

He pulled up at the foot of the steps and played a quick tattoo on the horn. Mark, standing with a group on the veranda, his back to the drive, spun on his heel, waved an arm at us and with a word to the others, ran down the steps.

"Hey, Jon," he said, "this is great. I phoned this morning to tell you I have something for you but the station said you'd be away all day."

He saw me then—really saw me, I mean. Not just as a person who'd come along with Jon and must be made welcome, but as the young woman with green eyes and copper hair who'd looked "just right" to him at the airport. We shared a moment of pleased recognition and his thoughts came through to me clearly. "Who says miracles don't happen? I thought you were a tourist that day and never expected to see you again and here you are in time for Claire's birthday party."

We smiled at each other like old friends.

Jon said, "Alix, this is Mark Kitteredge. You must get him to tell you about the ghost that walks in his garden. And Mark, this is Alix Bonney who is visiting St. Sebastian to collect material for a book on the Pompineaus. She is living in the chateau as a guest of the historical society."

"I envy you," he said, "I'd love to see the inside of the chateau. I tried once when Brandish was alive but was turned down flat. Le Sucrier belonged to the Pompineaus, too. It was a prosperous sugar plantation and they used to spend some time here each year. When Brandish was young, he lived here most of the time. Come on in—you'll stay for lunch of course?"

"Thanks, we'd love to. Right, Alix? If you've a drop of gin in the house we could do with a martini. We've spent the morning with Père Jules and a bottle of very sweet wine."

Mark grinned. "What you need is a Twin Special." He looked at me. "That's a double with two olives—a whimsy of the house."

The drinks were brought to us in Mark's study, a large room that had been built on to the back of the house. Stepping into it was like stepping into a pool of cool green water. Everything was green—the glass jalousies, the big straw rug covering most of the floor, the metal file cabinets, the large desk in the center of the room facing the door and the smaller one beside a window.

Mark put two wicker chairs near the big desk and a small table between them to hold our drinks. Perching himself on a corner of the desk he raised his glass and said "Skoal!"

The martini was very dry and very cold.

Mark set his glass down beside him, picked up a pack of cigarettes and dropped it into the pocket of his sport shirt.

"Notice anything unusual?" he asked. "No? I didn't think so. You weren't meant to." He took the pack from his pocket and tapped it with his finger. "Camouflage. Inside is a Wallace microphone. No cords. Nothing but a button on top that's made to look like a cigarette. Now, come over to the window." He turned a crank at the side of the window until the jalousies stood wide open. Outside, about fifty yards away from the house, was a helicopter with the words "Le Sucrier" painted in large letters on the side. "That's my private 'copter, though Jon has the use of it whenever he wishes. We were pilots together during our hitch with the army—matter of fact he rescued me once from a very sticky situation I'd got myself into. Don't ask him to tell you about it because he won't—you might call him a hero. Well, inside that 'copter is a reel-to-reel, battery-operated tape recorder with an FM tuner and a voice-activated microphone. I touch this button with my finger and our voices are immediately recorded over there on a tape."

"At this distance?" I asked. "It seems incredible."

"But it isn't. The microphone can transmit up to a couple of miles and with a stronger transmitter up to thirty or forty miles. When the recorder is set at its lowest speed the tape has three hours recording time."

"How do you shut it off? Is there another button on the microphone?"

"No, it's automatic. When the voice signals stop the recorder shuts off."

He handed the camouflaged microphone to Jon. "It's yours, Jonnie. You can use it to interview people with stage fright or catch criminals for the police department. You ought to have been a cop—you've proved it more than once."

Jon took a half-empty pack of Benson and Hedges from his shirt pocket and replaced it with the disguised microphone. "Thanks, Mark," he said. "Thanks a lot."

"De nada, amigo."

"Look, why don't we have some fun with it at the ball? I can circulate among the guests, get as many of their voices on tape as I can, and then, later, play it back to amuse them."

"Maybe it wouldn't," I laughed. "Oh, would some power the giftie gie us, to hear ourselves as others hear us!"

Mark put his arm around Jon's shoulders. "We'll do it! Let's go now and have lunch. I'm sorry Linda isn't here. She's at the beach with some friends. She likes to take a picnic lunch and make a day of it.'

In the dining room we served ourselves from a buffet and carried our plates to the table reserved for Mark.

Jon tasted his lobster salad. "Marvelous!" he said and asked, "How's Jim?"

"Fine. Lively as a jumping bean. He practically lives in the pool so Linda leaves him with the swimming instructor when she's away."

"Jim doesn't like the beach?"

"Loves it but I don't let him go unless I'm along. There are seldom any other children for him to play with—our guests usually leave theirs back home in the States—and he's too much on his own. A thermos jug of cocktails is part of the picnic lunch and people forget to look after a small boy. Jim's better off here in the pool."

I felt like asking "What's the matter with Linda looking after him?" but of course I didn't. What Jon had told me of her was answer enough. Women like Linda Kitteredge, selfish, vain, reckless, attention-seeking, are not apt to sacrifice their own pleasure to the demands of a bothersome child.

Mark may have sensed my unspoken criticism of Linda for he changed the subject quickly.

"I have been revising the plans for the annual ball. This year the guests will be asked to come in costumes patterned after the styles worn in the mid-eighteen hundreds. That should present no problem because I have checked the library and found that there are sketches on file of the fashions of that time. Then, to further the illusion that the clocks have been set back more than a century and that this is the actual ball to celebrate Claire's birthday, I will ask certain people to enact the roles of Jacques, Claire, the Governor and his aide, Knud Jensen. It was on this occasion, you know, that Claire and Knud met and fell in love."

He looked questioningly at us. "How does it strike you?"

I smiled. "It's a lovely idea."

"Great!" exclaimed Jon enthusiastically. "Whom do you have in mind for Jacques?"

Mark raised his iced tea glass in salute. "You," he said.

"Me? You must be out of your cotton-pickin' mind."

"Not at all. You've got the figure for it, tall and heavyset. Dressed in silk and with a curly, auburn wig on your head you'll make an impressive Jacques Pompineau."

Jon shook his head, but I thought he looked pleased.

Mark continued. "I've decided on Jens Andersen for the part of the governor. He was a Dane, like Jens, who also resembles him somewhat."

"Jens will make a splendid governor," I agreed. "He has the same poise and dignity and charm that are ascribed to the governor in the records. I'm sure he'll enjoy playing the part."

"And Claire?" asked Jon.

"I am hoping that I can persuade Alix to accept the role." He looked at me and spoke earnestly. "You are exactly right for the part. As Jon said, I have a ghost who walks in my garden. She is little, like you, and her hair is the same beautiful color of copper in the sun. Her eyes are green, and above them her brows, like yours, have a charming, fly-away look of a bird's wings. Will you bring that ghost to life, Alix? Please?"

"Go on, Alix, do it!" Jon held up his right hand and chuckled. "I hereby promise to be an indulgent and affectionate father."

I hesitated. "It sounds like fun and I know I'd enjoy it, but—"

"But?" prompted Mark.

"But maybe you should ask someone who's lived here longer than I have. I'm an outsider, almost a stranger. There must be lots of women who'd love to play the part of Claire. Perhaps your wife?"

Marks' lips tightened. "Linda can never be anyone but herself. To pretend to be someone different would bore her beyond measure. She'd rather be free to enjoy herself in her own way." Then, offsetting the slight hint of criticism in his words, he added lightly, "Wouldn't we all?"

"Well," I said, "if you're sure—"

"Indeed I am. You'll make a wonderful Claire. You and Jon will receive the guests in the drawing room. When the governor and his party arrive there'll be a dramatic moment when the aide, very romantic looking in his white uniform and gold braid, sees Claire for the first time and is obviously smitten."

Jon scowled. "I'll look at him like this. By the way, who's it to be?"

"Me," said Mark.

Now, looking back, I know that was the moment I fell in love with him.

His eyes, dark and unsmiling, held mine with a long, steady gaze that was like a caress.

Joyfully and irrevocably, I gave him my heart.

There were no guests in sight when we left the dining room. On the right of the long hall that ran from the front to the back of the house was a double drawing room with a folding door room-divider pushed back into the walls. Card tables had been set up, each with score pad and pencil and two decks of cards still in cellophane wrappers.

Jon took his key ring from his pocket. "I'll get the tape recorder and put it in the car. Be right back."

"I like this double room," I said. "With such high ceilings and so many windows it must be cool even on the hottest day."

"It is. With the two rooms thrown into one like this, it makes a fine ball-room, especially with a floor that is perfect for dancing."

"There is one just like it in the library of the chateau," I said. "The design is unusual."

"This floor was laid in preparation for Claire's birthday ball. It was made by a slave in the employ of the Pompineaus."

I nodded. "His name was Bozo. He made the one in the chateau, too. There is also a mahogany jewelry box with the same fleur-de-lis design, that we found in Claire's bedroom. He must have been a very skillful worker. There is a story that he ran away at the time of Claire's disappearance."

"He may have gone to search for her. Slaves often displayed great loyalty and devotion for their masters."

He touched my arm and drew my attention to a full length mirror in an ornate gilded frame on the opposite wall.

"Claire Pompineau may have looked into it many times. Perhaps a dim reflection of her lingers there still. Shall we look?"

We stood in front of the mirror, our two reflected faces smiling out at us.

"Do you see her?" he asked.

I said flippantly, "I see a red-haired girl in a green shirt and yellow slacks."

A girl in the mirror smiled back at me but not with my lips, for hers were gentler than mine and the sweetly curved chin below them had none of the stubborn quality evinced in my own. Her eyes were green, and her hair the same color as mine but instead of being tied back with a ribbon it fell loosely in curls over bare, white shoulders revealed by the low-cut bodice of a pink lace evening gown. My eyes blinked for an instant and the image was gone.

Mark's thoughts came through to me. "You belong here in this house, Alix. It welcomes you like an old friend. If I could, I would keep you here always. If I could? Hell, I'm more a slave than Bozo ever was, indentured like him, shackled by a promise I can never break, given on that night in a welter of blood and tears. Could I have forseen our meeting and the joy of falling in love with you, which, mea culpa, I have done, would I have given that promise?" A slight, barely audible sound, like a groan, came from his lips.

"Yes, by God, I would, even though I had known how great the sacrifice would be."

We stood, our arms touching, our eyes meeting in reflected, mutual unhappiness.

Jon's voice released us from the spell.

"Okay, Alix, let's get going. We haven't got too much time."

Mark walked with us to the car and stood with his arm resting on the window ledge beside me.

Impulsively I put my hand on his. "Come to Mon Domaine some day soon," I said. "You will enjoy going through the chateau and we will enjoy having you stay for lunch."

He turned his hand and closed his fingers around mine.

"Thank you," he said, and stopped. His fingers tightened on my hand.

A small, flashy, foreign car, spattering gravel like hailstones over everything within spattering distance, came streaking up the drive and stopped with a showy display of its driver's skill precisely at the center point of the broad, veranda steps. A door flew open and the red-haired child I had seen at the airport hurled himself at Mark and clutched him around the knees.

"Daddy, Daddy," he shrieked, "I've had a good time! André put me on his shoulders and swam way, way out, a long way, Daddy. I wasn't scared, honest. When we came in Mama gave me some of her drink and I liked it fine."

Mark put the boy aside firmly and stood waiting as Linda, following the boy, approached our car. She placed herself in front of Mark, her hands on her hips, her head uptilted, her lips parted in a mocking smile. Her bathing suit, still wet, was molded to her like a layer of white skin bisecting the bronze perfection of her body.

"Well?" she asked, a taunt in her voice.

I saw Mark's knuckles whiten as he gripped the door of the car.

"You gave me your promise not to take Jim to the beach." His voice was tense, every word icily distinct. "I was a damn fool to believe you."

She shrugged. "He's my son. Sometime you may forget that once too often."

I heard Mark catch his breath, saw his hand clench into a fist. Then, stooping quickly and rumpling the boy's hair he said, "Run along now, Jim, and get dressed. See you later."

Without a glance at us, Linda turned and walked away, swinging her hips, the boy trotting along beside her.

Jon started the car. Mark stepped back and raised a hand in reply to my "Goodbye now," and Jon's "Be seeing you, Mark."

No one was in the small foreign car as we passed. If André had been there he had lost no time in making himself scarce.

We drove back in silence to the little hotel where, only a few hours ago I had sat and sipped my fruit punch, blessedly unaware of the emotions that were to disturb me before the day was over.

Jon's only comment as we left Le Sucrier had been "If I were Mark I'd kill that woman."

Chapter 11

I awoke very early the next day. The room was cool with the freshness of early morning and spiced with the fragrance of charcoal burning in the kitchen of the carriage house where Delfina was preparing breakfast for Darwin and his two helpers.

I rose and went to the window, enjoying the smooth coolness of the tiled floor under my feet. In the east, the mountain ridge that rimmed the harbor stood darkly outlined against an unfolding fan of rose-colored clouds streaked with scarlet. As if my appearance had been a signal, a wafer-thin circlet of fiery gold emerged from behind the highest point of the ridge and rose majestically until, completely revealed, it poised, a glowing golden disk above the harbor and the hills.

I dressed hastily in shorts and a blouse and laced a pair of tennis shoes on my bare feet. I ran down the service stairs, unbolted the grille at the back of the house and stepped out onto the meadowlike stretch of ground on which the carriage house and a half-dozen box-shaped cabins were located. Under my feet the grass was dry and dusty and interspersed with small pale blue flowers. The double doors of the carriage house stood open and as I approached, Darwin came out and stood looking up at the sky, a toothpick dangling from his mouth. Ben and Luke, the two wiry, coffee-colored Puerto Ricans followed and, catching sight of me, grinned widely, their teeth very white amid the surrounding dark hedge of unshaven stubble.

"Buenos dias, Señorita," they chorused, and Darwin, discarding his toothpick said, "Mo-nin', Miss Alix. Dee sun be plenty hot 'fore long."

Behind him, silhouetted against the light at the open back door, I could see Delfina standing rigidly, her head thrust forward, listening.

I said good morning and walked to the margin of the field where the cliff sloped to a small bay and a crescent of rocky, timber-strewn beach below. Several men in tattered shorts moved about on a dock to which a couple of fishing boats were moored. A few women stood idly in the doorways of wooden shacks while naked children played at their feet.

I continued my walk, skirting the edge of the cliff, stopping to peer in at the open doors of the small cabins I passed. The faded brick walls were crumbling in places and the single step in front of each door was worn thin. Originally cabins for the house slaves, according to Jens, they now stood empty except for one or two that contained garden tools, sacks of fertilizer, paint cans and the like. One, considerably larger than the others and located at some distance from them, looked as if it might have been a store house with its arched, closely shuttered windows set high in the walls and its massive iron door, approached by a ramp. The door, I saw as I walked up the ramp, was standing ajar. I put out my hand to open it, but stopped suddenly aware of a warning sense of danger somewhere behind me. I turned swiftly. Nothing stirred on the faint path my feet had pressed into the grass. Beyond, at the coachhouse, Delfina, crouching with her back to me, picked something from the ground and stood, her head thrown back so far that her braids like long, black snakes, hung far below her waist. Three times, with a pause between each, she raised her right arm and threw something—a stone, I thought—over her left shoulder. Then, gathering her long skirt in her hands she ran, swift as an island mongoose, across the field and disappeared into the chateau. For the hundredth time or more since my coming to Mon Domaine I asked myself why this strange West Indian woman should bear me ill will even to the point of using witchcraft against me, for certainly in the performance I had just witnessed she had appeared to be casting a spell of some kind on me. If so, any obeah she had used against me had resulted so far in nothing more than an occasional bad headache. She's probably not very good at it, I thought.

I went into the building that once had been so carefully designed for protection against incursion. It contained only one room—bare floor, four walls and the roof for a ceiling. In the opposite wall was another door, also standing ajar, which in spite of its great size and weight opened easily and noiselessly to my touch. Curious, I rubbed my fingers over one of the hinges and found that it had been recently oiled. By Darwin? Why?

I stepped outside and walked to the edge of the cliff. Beyond and far below was the sea stretching into seemingly limitless space, blue like the sky and sprinkled with sparks of light like diamond chips winking in the sun. At my feet the cliff plunged steeply, covered with a dense thicket of thorn-covered bushes interlaced with leafless, orange-colored vines. Through it lay a barely discernible trail, so overgrown that it would have escaped my notice if it had not been for the presence, at intervals, of branches that had been hacked off and thrown aside; branches on which the leaves had not entirely withered. This, I imagined, must be the third means of approach between the fort and the chateau, described by Jens as impassable. It had been in use, however, and recently for, looking closely, I could see fresh black soil marking the spots where bushes had been cleared away. Why on earth anyone would choose such a precipitous path in preference to the newer and easier pirate trail was beyond my understanding,—unless, perhaps, from an urgent need to remain invisible? And why, if the business was legitimate, should it be necessary for anyone using it to keep out of sight? To search for hidden treasure in the fort? A secret room inside the walls?

A picture flashed into my mind—myself seated in the library, reading a letter in which the splendors of the chateau were described. The words came back to me. "I suspect the existence of a secret room filled with chests overflowing with jewels and coins of gold and silver, for without such treasure how could the Pompineaus have continued to live for so many years in splendor rivalling that of a royal potentate?"

I, too, had suspected the existence of a secret room, a tomb in which the bodies of Claire and her lover might have been hidden, but the thought had never occurred to me that it might be located in the old fort. Wasn't it logical to assume that pirate loot had at times been stashed in the fort until some chosen hour when, under cover of darkness, it could be removed to the chateau? And if indeed, a secret room did exist within the thick walls of the fort, wouldn't it also be logical to assume that it had been chosen by Jacques Pompineau as a repository for his guilty secret?

With growing excitement I thought back to the scene in the library at the moment before I had lost consciousness. Cash Hawks and Jacques Pompineau struggling for control of the deadly weapon, already discharged, which still in Jacques' hand, emitted a wisp of smoke from its muzzle. Knud Jensen, his white uniform stained with blood, lying dead at their feet, his body held within the circle of Claire's arms. And she, her long, auburn hair spread like a veil over her lover's face, her anguish stilled in death, an ugly, gaping wound between her white shoulders staining the lace and rosebuds of her lovely gown.

Beyond that, I knew nothing.

I closed my eyes against the serene beauty of my surroundings, the better to hold in my mind the picture of that resurrected moment in time. And then, like film projected onto a screen, the events that followed after the tragedy were revealed to me.

Jacques stood, rigid with shock, stunned by the awful realization that with his own hand he had slain the daughter whom he had loved above all else in the world. The pistol dropped from his fingers, and as Cash Hawks bent to retrieve it, Jacques uttered a harsh cry that seemed to have been wrenched from his throat.

"Go!" he screamed, almost choking on the word.

Hawks, silent, without a backward glance, pushed open one of the French windows and disappeared into the night.

Then Jacques, not taking his eyes from the bodies, backed around the table to the wall. Closing his hand on an embroidered bell pull hanging there tugged the heavy tassel three times. He was still there, his arms limp at his sides when steps sounded from the foyer and a man entered the room. I knew by the color of his skin and the deferential manner in which he inclined his head to Jacques that he was Bozo, the slave.

Jacques raised his hand and pointed.

With a cry of grief so poignant that it can never be erased from my memory, the slave threw himself on his knees beside Claire while great tears rained down his face and fell on her bright hair.

Jacques spoke and his voice was toneless like that of a person totally deaf.

"You will put them in the vault," he said. "No trace must remain."

His body sagged against the table, his hand shaking violently as he removed the stopper from a full decanter near the one that he and Cash Hawks had so recently emptied.

The slave stumbled to his feet. He walked to the table and put his hand on the dark, polished surface.

"I obey," he said.

Now bright light stabbed at my eyelids and a scarlet haze came between me and the dreadful scene. My eyes hurt as if they had been staring directly into the sun. I opened them and quickly shielded them with my hand from the brilliant glare of the water reflecting the concentrated rays of the sun.

How long had I been standing here? An hour, at least, must have passed since I had left the house. I would put off searching the fort until after breakfast when Abby would be settled as usual in the cool reception room with her lists of furniture and the stack of antiques magazines that she used for reference. I would go by way of the terrace steps and examine the fort as I should have done soon after the vision of the pirates. Had that vision, like my father's voice directing me to the fateful letter, been meant to direct me to the hiding place of Claire's body? More than ever I was convinced that until her bones were found and decently interred, there would be no peace within the chateau.

I took a step backward and froze.

To my left, farther along the side of the cliff where the

newer pirate trail rose from the fort to the base of the conical tower, I saw a spot of bright color moving rapidly downward amid the shrubbery and low-branched trees that almost hid it from sight. The color was unmistakable, the bright gypsy red that Delfina always wore. Why, when she should be preparing breakfast for Abby and me was she hurrying stealthily to the fort? Purely by chance I had seen her cast some sort of spell and then run into the chateau. It would have taken her less than a minute to reach the base of the tower and start down the trail. But why? To carry out some further indispensable condition of the spell?

Without hesitation, though disagreeably aware of the possibility of a bad fall, I began the treacherous descent. I had taken only a few steps when a stone rolled under my foot and threw me off balance. In a desperate attempt to save myself from falling I threw out my arms and clutched the thorny bushes beside me for support. The pain was excruciating but I hung on until I was steady again on my feet. My hands had been cut cruelly and were slippery with blood but forcing myself to stand the pain I pulled out several thorns that had broken off in my hands and wiped the blood on my shorts and blouse. Delfina was still in sight. Cautiously, and with a wary eye for loose stones or treacherous, trailing vines to trap my feet, I made my way down the cliff, often slipping, sometimes falling, scratched by thorns, and stung by swarms of almost invisible gnats. Once my foot slid into a loop of orange vine that lay tangled in the underbrush. I felt it tighten like a noose around my ankle. Completely off balance, I toppled and fell like a tree axed at the roots. Shaken, but apparently uninjured, I twisted around and sat up, tearing at the coils of vine that were cutting into my flesh. I thrust my fingers between the blood-stained vine and my lacerated flesh and pulled with the strength of desperation. When I had freed my foot I struggled upright and putting my weight on it gingerly hobbled the remaining distance to where the trail terminated in a short flight of stone steps leading down to a stony crossing. Opposite was the fort, starkly outlined against the sky. The steps, old and crumbling, matted with vines and screened by spreading branches of thickly foliaged shrubs, were a perfect place from which to survey it. Careful to make no sound I let myself down on the top step, glad that my clothes were the same color as the greenery that sheltered me from view. My ankle had begun to swell and was hurting abominably and my head ached with the stabbing pain that I had come to associate with Delfina's obeah.

From my position I could see into the roofless interior of the ancient gray fortress, and, through the arched openings cut into the walls, to the sea beyond. A rough stone track, partly overgrown with weedy grass and broken at intervals by shallow steps, passed in front of the empty doorway and descended to the level of the gun emplacement that rounded the base of the walls and faced the harbor. Not a sound disturbed the profound silence. Nothing stirred, not even the large green lizard sunning itself on the parapet. No splash of gypsy red disturbed the harmony of green and weathered gray and the blue of sea and sky. Delfina's errand, which had appeared to be urgent, must have been accomplished in a matter of minutes for I could see no sign of her in the great open space within the walls or on the bare stony ground outside. In all probability, I thought, she was already back on the trail, hurrying to reach the chateau before her absence should be noted.

Confident that I was alone, I went down the steps, crossed the track and stood on the old stone platform where my ancestors had trained their cannons on any rival pirate ship rash enough to venture into the harbor.

Eager to begin my search for a hidden room, I did not follow the curve of the platform around the corner of the wall. Had I done so I would, as I now know, have seen the iron ring that had been sunk centuries before into the paving, and the long rope knotted through it to secure a small motor boat lying close inshore. And I would have seen the two who stood quarreling in a patch of shade close to the wall. What would have happened if I had rounded the corner and come upon them unawares? Would they have killed me then? And afterward flung my body over the low parapet to the jagged rocks below? But I had not turned the corner. Instead, I had gone up the shallow steps to the gaping doorway of the fort.

I went inside, thinking as I crossed the threshold of the vast, empty room of the many who had crossed there before me: first soldiers and pirates, then later the smugglers who had come by night with the liquor, silks, and laces that would line their pockets and those of the Pompineaus with gold.

At my left, beyond the rubble that had once been a dividing wall, I could see a smaller room which in my imagination, had been occupied by the officer in command of the fort.

At my right an iron gate sagged on its hinges across an opening in the thick wall. I crossed to it and looked down at a flight of narrow stone steps and another iron gate at the foot.

A muted sound of voices raised in argument came from somewhere close by though not, as I had first thought, from below the stairs. Curious to locate the sound, I went to a window in the wall facing the sea and leaned as far as I could over the broad sill. The voices came from directly under the window but because of the width of the sill I could not see who stood beneath it.

Delfina's voice came, sharp with anger. "I tell you once more she is the one. Always she is looking, looking. If she has seen the trail she will follow it here. That is why I have come running to warn you. You must go. Now!"

"You were a damn fool to leave the door unlocked."

The man's voice gave me no clue to his identity. In fact I was positive that I had never heard it before.

Delfina's reply was sulky. "I'd been up nearly the whole night helping you search. I was tired. I had to get back before Darwin woke and missed me from the bed. How was I to know that the girl would be out that early before I had time to lock it?"

"You could have stopped her from entering, couldn't you?" He gave a short, ugly laugh. "Or could you? I wonder."

"I tried, I swear I did. I threw the stones and said the words and went away without looking back, exactly the way it has to be done. But I heard the door creak so she must have gone in."

"Damn it, you've lied to me all along about your power to cast spells. Not one of them has worked."

"I have not lied. Something protects her. Something that knows who she is."

"Who she is! Who she is! How can you be so sure?"

"I tell you a hundred times already and you do not believe. The old man talked to himself when he was drunk. I listened. Sometimes all night I listened at the door. He say only one will survive the curse: a woman."

"The ramblings of a drunkard!"

"No! Because it is not only to himself that he talked. Jacques Pompineau was in that room with him. I swear it."

The man snorted his disgust. "You are a greater fool than I thought. No one with an ounce of brains believes that the dead come back. For God's sake don't waste any more time with such talk. This is what you are to do: take everything away with you. Hide it in the bushes along the trail. Tonight, after dark, go back for it. And do not forget again to lock the door. To be on the safe side I will stay away for awhile."

"Not for long. You will have to get rid of the young woman soon. I will help you."

The man laughed. "With your spells? No, thank you. I know a better way. Quicker, too."

A door opened and closed. Footsteps approached the smaller room on stairs I had not known were there.

I pushed myself back from my awkward position on the window sill and looked around desperately for a place to hide. The footsteps were closer now. There was only one place where I could hope to remain unseen. I would have to go through the iron gate and down the steps, wherever they might lead. I had forgotten my twisted ankle. Under my weight the foot doubled over and I fell, unable to hold back a gasp of pain. I bit down hard on my lip and held my breath, expecting to be discovered in the next minute. The footsteps stopped. Whoever was on the stairs was standing there listening. If I was going to be killed I would not just lie there and wait for it. I flipped over on my face, put my weight on my forearms and snaked across the floor with more speed than I would have thought possible. I was through the gate and on the stairs when the sound of the footsteps was resumed. At the bottom I stood up gingerly and found that the ankle, though painful, would support me. In front of me was another gate like the one at the top of the stairs. I looked through the bars into a cell-like room that smelled of damp and the accumulated dirt of years upon years. The gate moved easily and without a sound as if it had been recently oiled.

Inside the room, I shut the gate but found that it could be secured only by an iron bar on the outside. Light from the sun-flooded room at the top of the stairs threw my figure in silhouette against the opposite wall, striping it with the bold, black bars of the gate. High above it a single window, no more than a slit for ventilation had been cut into the stone. On the floor, drawn slightly away from the wall was a camp cot made up with sheets and a plump pillow in a clean white pillowcase. Beside it, lying open on the floor, was a black leather attaché case containing toilet articles. The top sheet on the cot had been turned back in a an even fold in the center of which, matching the pillowcase, was a single, embroidered fleur-de-lis. I stared at it with as much indignation as if I were already the mistress of the chateau. Who, I wanted to know, besides myself and Abby, had permission to use the exquisite bed linens we had found stored in great, carved chests, still retaining a faint fragrance of the ylang-ylang blossoms scattered among them by hands long since reduced to dust? In the act of bending over for a closer look my eye caught a movement in the rectangle of light that had framed my silhouette. Instantly my brain signalled a warning that my body, paralyzed with sudden fear, refused to heed. Helplessly I watched the shadow of a man raise his arm. The rock in his hand had a jagged edge. He was no stranger—I had seen him before, poised as he was now, but wielding a different kind of weapon.

Reason, and the strength to act returned to me in a flash. In the split second before the large rock struck, I jerked my head sideways. While this did not prevent a painful injury it did succeed in deflecting the blow enough to defeat the deadly purpose of my would-be assassin.

I seemed to be sinking into a pit that was utterly devoid of light but filled with a low humming that gradually resolved itself into broken sounds recognizable as words. By instinct I knew that I must listen and understand—that I must fight against the darkness of the pit and will myself to retain consciousness. Hazily I wondered why. And saw, as if imprinted on the retina of my eyes, a splash of sunshine on a wall and the dark shadow of a slim figure with its arm upraised.

And knew, beyond the shadow of a doubt who it was that had murdered my cousin Brandy!

Chapter 12

The back of my head hurt horribly. I touched it gingerly and felt the wetness and stickiness of blood on my fingers. The edge of a stone step was cutting into the back of my neck and the rest of my body sprawled on the stone floor like a discarded rag doll. I raised my head and managed to sit up despite the dizziness and nausea that sickened me. In front of me was an iron gate that I remembered though it was not now standing open as I had last seen it. I limped over it, my ankle hurting almost as much as my head, and discovered that it was locked. Through the bars I looked at an empty room. The camp cot with its covering of fine linen was gone, as well as the black leather case that had been on the floor beside it. I raised my eyes and saw, projected on the opposite wall the blackness of my own shadow. Had I not glimpsed that other, sinister shadow in time I would now be lying dead. Shuddering, I turned my back on that dark reminder of my brush with death.

Slowly and painfully, I made my way to the top of the stairs and crossed the big, empty room to the window where, not long ago, I had stood and listened to the quarrelsome voices below. Beyond, in the harbor, the Goose took off from the water and headed for the hazy outline of St. Croix. Judging by the position of the sun this must be the usual nine o'clock flight to the neighboring island. In that case Darwin must have left already to pick up the mail from the post office in St. Sebastian. If I could make it to the landing before his return I could ride in the jeep with him to the chateau. But first I must find a way to get down to the shore.

Outside, at the front of the fort, the shallow steps led down on the left to the gun emplacement below which there was a sheer drop to the water's edge. On the right they climbed uphill past the beginning of the trail down which Delfina had hastened, and terminated at a level of ground overgrown with weeds.

It was an effort for me to lift myself from one step to another. The sun beat down on my head, and the ankle I had twisted was swelling over my shoe like yeast dough rising in a bowl. There were only eight steps to negotiate but when I reached the last one I felt as if I had descended Everest. A little breeze blowing in from the sea loosened the hair that had stuck to my wet forehead, and cooled my hot cheeks. Ahead, a little path wound through the weeds for a short distance, curved to the edge of the cliff and dipped over it. I walked slowly, putting my weight on the good foot and barely touching the ground with the other. Off to my right I could see the Caribbean and a white ship heading in toward the barbor. At the docks three cruise ships were already moored and another lay at anchor in mid-harbor. Several small boats skittered over the smooth water: among them I recognized the harbor master's launch on its way to the incoming ship. At the edge of the cliff I took a deep breath and started down, expecting with each step to fall and roll like a barrel the rest of the way. Below lay the narrow, stony beach I had hoped to find and a little cove in which a small boat would not be visible from the waterfront of St. Sebastian. Down on the beach I found the going easier and managed to reach the dock with a few minutes to spare before Darwin's arrival with the mail. I sank down on the hot, concrete floor and tried to sort out my confused recollections of the moments that had followed the attack. I remembered feeling the blow, which, as I discovered later, had gashed my head instead of crushing it in. I remembered too, that before losing consciousness I had heard Delfina's voice.

"You've killed her," she said. "For once you've taken my advice."

The man, whose voice I had heard earlier, spoke sharply. "Don't touch her, you fool. You'll get blood on you."

"I want to make sure she's dead. Turn her over and listen for a heart beat."

"There's no time. That blow would have brained an ox. While I drag her to the stairs you strip the bed and fold it so I can put it in the boat. Take the sheets with you and hide them in the bushes. I'll stay away for awhile."

Rough hands seized my ankles and pulled me off the bed. Agonizing pain shot through my head as it struck the floor. The next minute could well have been my last had I not been able to stifle the scream that would have betrayed the fact that I was still alive. I must have lost consciousness then because no memory remained of having been dragged across the floor. I was looking at the grime that had been ground into my clothing when I became aware of the boat approaching the dock with Darwin standing in the prow, a long rope dangling from his hand, his expression a mixture of incredulity, dismay and alarm.

"Miss Alix!" he exclaimed as the boat nudged the dock. "You is hurt! All dat blood! You can' rightly stan' up—jes stay put till I come 'n' help you."

He tossed a small canvas bag stamped "Mon Domaine" to the dock, jumped out and made the boat fast to the iron ring set into the concrete.

When we were in the jeep he said, "Look lak you hadda bad fall. Wha' you hit you' head on?"

I had already decided on a plausible explanation of my injuries that would not alarm Abby, so I said, "On solid rock, Darwin. I twisted my ankle and fell down some stairs in the fort. I'm not hurt very much but I seem to have bled a lot, don't I?"

"A plenty. Miss Abby gonna be real scare when she see you. Dat old fort be fallin' to pieces—'tain' safe to walk dere no more."

"Not safe at all," I agreed.

Which is what Abby said, too, after she'd heard my story about a fall down a flight of stairs.

"I can't understand why you went to the fort alone.

You could have lain there for hours before anyone thought to look there for you."

"I'm sorry," I said. "It was such a pretty morning and the fort looked so interesting down by the water that I couldn't resist an impulse to go and take a look at it."

I had gone straight from the jeep to the open court where Abby liked to have breakfast. She was spreading some of Delfina's mango marmalade on a piece of toast when she heard my step and looked up apologetically.

"I couldn't wait," she began. "I was so hungry—"

The knife fell from her hand and in an instant she was out of her chair and hurrying to me.

"What has happened, Alix? Are you all right? Let me see where you're hurt. You must get off that ankle—it looks bad. Come!"

She put her arm around me and was helping me walk to a chair when Delfina came from the pantry with fresh toast. As she entered between the columns she saw me and stood stock-still, her tawny cheeks turning a muddy gray as the blood drained from them. Her eyes were wide and frightened as they took in my limp figure, the blood on my face and the ugly red splotches on the shoulders of my grimy blouse. As the plate she was holding fell and shattered on the floor she opened her mouth to scream but suddenly covered it with her hands and ran from the court. She was back in the pantry with the door slammed shut behind her before Abby and I found our voices.

"Good Lord!" I gasped, remembering that Delfina had believed me to be dead.

"What made her look at you like that?" Abby's arm tightened around me. "She seemed to take leave of her senses, yet I'd have said it would take a lot more than the sight of blood to scare the wits out of that one. Come, sit down and tell me where you've been and how you got hurt. Here, dear, drink some coffee. You look as if you need it."

So I gave her a carefully edited account of my morning's adventures. I told of finding the original trail and how, full of curiosity, I had followed it to the fort. I described the worn, stone steps leading down to a cell behind an iron gate, said I had fallen and that, when I came to I was lying at the foot of the stairs with a sprained ankle and a lump the size of a hen's egg on my aching head.

I hated having to keep back so much of the truth about my visit to the fort but to me the fight against evil on Mon Domaine had become a very personal one in which I was determined not to involve Abby and Jens. To face by myself the fact that my life was in constant jeopardy was one thing; to permit two people whom I loved to share that knowledge with me was quite another.

So when Abby said, "You're not accident prone, Alix, and never were. When other children were falling out of trees and breaking their arms or tumbling off their bikes and knocking their teeth out you were doing the same stunts and getting off without a scratch. If what happened to you this morning had occurred here in the house I might put some stock in Jens' talk about evil spirits."

I answered, "You'd be a great goose if you did!"

But later, when Jens had listened to my story of the fall and exclaimed, *"Jeg kan ikke lide dat!* No, I do not like it! I do not like it at all!" I agreed silently and speaking only to myself said, "Neither do I. Believe me, neither do I!"

Chapter 13

The telephone that had been installed in a cubbyhole under the stairs rang insistently. I frowned and hurriedly signed my name on an airmail order to White's in Augusta for trimming for my gown for Claire's birthday ball.

By the time I reached the phone Abby was already there speaking enthusiastically to someone on the other end of the line.

"Of course you may bring him to see us," she was saying. "I'd love to meet him. Alix says he is charming. No, it won't matter a bit if you can't get here until late in the day. Why not come over with Jens for cocktails and stay for dinner? Darwin will have the boat at the waterfront at five. Will that be convenient for you? Good! We'll look forward to seeing you. Alix? Yes, she's right here. Hold on, please."

She handed me the receiver, said, "Jon wants to talk to you," and went away, smiling.

"Hi, Jon," I said. "I'm glad to hear you're coming over."

"Hi! That's what I want to talk to you about. Mark flew over this morning to bring me some news and I've asked Abby if we may pay you a visit."

My heart gave a leap. "How nice!" I said, trying to keep

the excitement out of my voice. "That day in St. Croix I promised to take him through the chateau whenever he happened to be in St. Sebastian. Now I can take you both through at the same time. You really haven't seen much more than Claire's room."

"That's fine, Alix, but that's not why we're coming. Mark has some information that I'd like him to tell you in person. Listen, sugar, I want your permission to tell him why it's especially important for you to hear what he's just finished telling me. Okay?"

"Must you, Jon? Didn't we agree to keep it quiet until . . . ?" I hesitated, wondering whether an operator might be listening in.

Jon spoke quickly. "Yes, we did, but please take my word for it that Mark ought to be told the facts. You needn't be afraid he'll talk."

"That's not it. I'm sure I can trust him the same as I trust you. I guess I'm overly cautious because there's so much at stake. Someone, you know, might just consider me expendable."

"Don't be flippant—it's no joking matter. Well, do I have your permission?"

"I suppose so. If you think it's necessary I'll go along with it."

"Good girl! See you tonight."

I hung up the receiver, went into the court and sat on the pink marble ledge of the fountain watching the goldfish and tiny mosquito fish dart in and out among the lily pads in the basin. Like them my thoughts darted restlessly.

What kind of information had Mark given Jon? Why should it be important for Mark to know my real identity? Why did I wish he didn't have to know? Wasn't it because it would be only natural for him to wonder whether I had inherited not only Claire's appearance but also the cruel, rapacious nature of the Pompineaus? Would I read that in his eyes—or hear it in his thoughts—tonight?

At that point I tried to stop thinking but it was no use. I could no more put Mark out of my mind than I could stop myself from breathing. He was married, not happily, perhaps, but still he was the husband of another woman and the father of a little boy who loved and trusted him. What right had I to consider my happiness of more importance than theirs? What reason had I to hope that some day I would walk in Linda's shoes? Hadn't I heard Mark's unspoken declaration that he was bound irrevocably by a promise he would not break? Why then dream dreams that could never come true?

By the time the three men arrived that afternoon I had made the decision that I would never add to Mark's unhappiness by giving him the slightest reason to suspect that I, too, was committed to a love that was hopeless.

We sat under the gaily striped awning of Abby's improvised veranda. Jens mixed the cocktails while Abby added tiny Danish meatballs to a spicy sauce that was bubbling fragrantly in a silver chafing dish. She, after so many years of dull routine in the dreary atmosphere of my father's house was now thoroughly enjoying her new surroundings and happy way of life. I wished that Louise Boneffet could have been present with her brushes and tubes of paint to capture on canvas the magic of that hour as the bright rays of the setting sun slowly faded and the first star appeared in a sky afloat with fleecy pink clouds.

I felt that Mark was watching me and turned my head quickly, realizing as our eyes met that I had responded to his thought as instantly as if he had called my name aloud. I did not look away—I couldn't—and perhaps he saw in my eyes the answers to the questions in his mind.

"Alix, can you guess that I love you? Can you imagine what it is like to fall in love—really in love—and know that such happiness is denied you?" Then, very earnestly, "Don't ever love me, my dear one. Promise you won't. Because it can only lead to sorrow."

I longed to cry, "But I do, Mark. I love you so very, very much!"

So much for my noble decision!

Jens was now refilling our glasses and when he finished Jon took an envelope from his pocket and laid it on the table before him.

He said, "I have here a document that Mark has asked me to read to you. First he will explain how it came to be written. Mark?"

He took a sip of his cocktail and looked expectantly at Mark.

"It's rather a long story," said Mark. "It began when one of my guests, a very wealthy politician, a widower with a sixteen-year-old daughter, came to me and asked for information about another guest whose name is André Darcy."

"Darcy!" exclaimed Jens.

"Exactly—the man who claims to be the heir to the Pompineau estate, which as all of us here know is impossible."

"Shall we say improbable?" Jens asked. "Louis may have had children by a previous marriage before he arrived in Augusta and built a home for his bride."

"Have patience, Jens, we'll come to that later. Anyway, I told my guest that I knew nothing of Darcy beyond the fact that he had first come to Le Sucrier for a weekend at the invitation of my wife who had become acquainted with him in San Sebastian. At the end of the weekend Darcy had decided to remain and had engaged a room for an indefinite length of time. My guest became agitated and disclosed that his daughter was infatuated with Darcy. She had been accustomed all her life to get whatever she wanted and now she wanted Darcy who, as far as her father knew, had nothing to offer beyond his charm and a boasted claim to an estate that had yet to be proved authentic. He said he had reason to suspect that Darcy's expenses were not being paid out of his own pocket but were being shared among some of the women guests who, like his daughter, were infatuated to the point of folly."

"Damn fools!" Jens exploded. "What did the father propose to do?"

"Above everything else he wished to avoid publicity. He was sure that Darcy was a fraud and a fortune hunter but had no way to prove it. Any overt action on his part could lead to a suit for defamation of character, so he decided to have Darcy investigated by the Pinkertons."

"Good!" said Jens. "An excellent decision."

Abby took a deep breath. "Did he carry it out?"

"Yes, he did. His orders were to spare no expense and to collect every bit of information about Darcy and his background that could be obtained. You never met him, did you Jens?"

"Nej. He has avoided me as if I were the devil."

"Lucky you!" I thought and touched the still-tender spot on my head where I had been hit.

"So what happened?" asked Abby.

"This," said Mark. He picked up the envelope and tapped it on the edge of the table.

Abby's face flushed with excitement. She took Jens' hand and held it tightly. "They got the proof!" she exclaimed.

Mark handed the envelope to Jon.

"I'd like you all to hear the report," he said.

He picked up his glass and raised it slightly to me. The words came, clear as the crystal he held in his hand, but only I could hear them.

"I love you, Alix Pompineau," he said.

Jon took a thick sheaf of papers from the envelope and unfolded them on the table. Then he glanced at his wristwatch, raised his eyebrows and looked at Mark.

"It's getting late and this report is lengthy. Wouldn't it be better, Mark, to leave it until after dinner? Or why don't I summarize it now and leave the details for later?"

Jens nodded emphatically, "Ja, that is the best way. Otherwise the suspense will spoil our appetites for dinner."

"Oh, no," protested Abby. "We're going to have . . ."

Mark raised his hand. "Don't tell me. I want to be surprised. Okay, Jon give us a summary."

Jon leaned back, laced his fingers together and rested his chin on them. After a minute he began to talk.

"The Pinkerton man who was engaged by Mark's guest had no difficulty in finding the small town near Paris where Darcy had lived before coming to St. Sebastian. He found the house, a small, neat cottage and talked with Darcy's mother and three sisters. They were fond of him but admitted that he liked to gamble and whenever he could afford it played for high stakes. He was popular with women of all ages and did not hesitate to accept expensive gifts from them. One day at breakfast while reading the newspaper he had become excited, thrown down the paper and left the house hurriedly. His mother looked at everything on the page he had been reading but aside from one small paragraph found nothing that, in her opinion, could have affected him so strangely. When questioned by the detective she said that the paragraph had been about a low-priced cruise to the Caribbean and had given the itinerary. She had not been surprised when, a week later her son had told her that he was going for a short pleasure trip and would write to her. She did not remember the itinerary but recalled the name St. Sebastian when it was suggested to her."

Jon picked up the papers and spread them open like a fan.

"Most of these deal with the detective's efforts to trace Darcy's lineage back to the great-grandfather who, he claims, was Louis Pompineau. Since we are summarizing, it is enough to say now that the trail apparently came to an end with the grandfather, one René Darcy who had been a silk merchant in Lyons. Then, purely by chance, the detective entered a second-hand book store and picked up an old school book. On the flyleaf was written Emilie Sebastian and below it the name of a convent. René Darcy's wife had been named Emilie—it said so on their gravestones and her grandson, André, had been startled by something he saw in the newspaper which could have been the name of the Caribbean island, St. Sebastian. Acting on a hunch, the Pinkerton man located the convent in a suburb of the city and paid it a visit. He was told that a girl named Emilie Sebastian had graduated from their school and had lived in a section of the town that had been destroyed by fire many years ago. He examined the few records that had escaped the flames. Nowhere was there any mention of the name Sebastian. Then in the town library he saw a framed picture of the dedication of the original library building. Next door to it was a shop with a sign above the door that said B. Sebastian, Cabinet Maker. On the steps stood the proprietor, B. Sebastian, father of Emilie who married René Darcy who was the grandfather of André Darcy."

Jon paused to draw a photostatic copy of a picture from among the papers on the table.

"Here is your proof," he said. "André Darcy's great-grandfather was a black man."

Chapter 14

Early the next morning Mark returned to St. Croix. From Claire's window in the tower I watched the helicopter until it disappeared into the blue haze that shrouded the distant outline of the island.

Last night we had lingered long over our coffee and cognac in Abby's pavilion. The hills, extended like arms to enfold the harbor, wore bracelets of winking lights and higher on the slopes some scattered lights gleamed like brooches pinned to their softly rounded bosoms. The water front had adorned itself with necklaces of colored lights and high over the town a star-studded sky, wore the slender sickle of a new moon as a golden tiara.

Fanciful? Yes. But isn't that part of being in love?

Ever since dinner we had been discussing the report that Jon had summarized for us.

Mark said, "It would be interesting to know how Bozo made his way to France. He may have had friends among the crew of the freighters that visited the island regularly. For a price they may have been willing to smuggle him aboard. It's possible that he stole the money from Jacques; he would have needed enough to live on until he could find work somewhere far from here. He had no name other than Bozo so we can suppose he chose Sebastian because it symbolized the home and security he'd enjoyed so many years."

"Yes," I agreed, "that's probably the way it happened. Later he married and had a daughter. Her son was André's father who died when André was still a child. Mrs. Darcy didn't know much about her husband's family, did she?"

"No, really very little. She did finally recall an interesting thing. Her husband had told the child bedtime stories that he had heard from his own grandfather. They were long stories and full of details that she had forgotten but she did remember that there had been an island in them and a castle with a secret room. There had been two brothers who quarreled and one had gone away to die of a broken heart."

I nodded. "Yes, Bozo would have remembered all that."

"The detective asked if she remembered the name of the island and she said no. However, when she'd seen in the paper that there is an island named St. Sebastian she'd remembered that her husband's grandfather had been named Sebastian, and wasn't that a strange coincidence?"

"So that's where André got so much information about the Pompineaus," said Abby. "I've wondered about that. By the way, how did the detective get Mrs. Darcy to talk so freely?"

"He told her he was looking for the missing heir to a fortune and that there was a possible chance it might be her son. He said it was better not to mention this to André if she wrote to him because it might raise hopes that could turn out to be false."

"Udmoerket! Ja, that was very good! Your anxious guest got his money's worth, didn't he? How did his daughter take it?"

"She went back home with him as meek as a lamb. He was so relieved that he gave me a copy of the report for my files. You should have it, Jens, of course. Will you show it to Tom Turner right away or wait awhile?"

Before he answered, Jens poured cognac into our empty glasses. Then he said slowly, "I think I should do nothing at this time. We know that his pretensions are no threat to Alix's claim any longer though he is not aware of that. Give him enough rope and he'll hang himself. What is your opinion, Alix?"

I shivered, remembering the abortive attempt to kill me. I had no doubt about the identity of my attacker or that he would strike again. True, he had abandoned his hideout in the fort, but might he not return at any time to continue his stealthy search by night for the secret room? If he found it wouldn't he make sure this time that I did not live to dispute his claim? Nevertheless, in spite of the risk, I wanted the terms of Brandy's will to be carried out to the letter. André Darcy as a claimant, rightful or not, must have his chance to appear in Tom Turner's office on the appointed day.

I took a sip from my glass before I answered. "In two months Brandy's specified year of waiting will be up. I say let André have those two months. His position will be no better then than it is now."

Jon moved restlessly in his chair. "I think we should get the bastard now and be done with it."

"Nej, Jon. He is legally entitled to a hearing. Let him have it."

Little by little the bright colored lights on the waterfront had winked out. The town was like a dark checkerboard marked off in squares by criss-crossed rows of white street lights.

The evening was over. Our chairs scraped noisily on the wide stone step as we pushed them back and stood saying our good nights. Jens whistled and the headlights of the jeep flashed on in front of the house where Darwin had been waiting.

Mark put his hand on my arm as the others started across the lawn. I turned my head and tried to see his face. The pavilion was in deep shadow. I could not see him and I was glad because my eyes, looking into his, would have betrayed the love that I had vowed to keep hidden.

"Alix!" He spoke softly with his lips close to my ear. "Give me this one minute here alone with you. I love you, Alix. I have no right to tell you. Try to forget, if you can."

"Can love forget?" I asked.

I turned my head so that my cheek brushed against his lips. His arms closed around me and held me close. Our kiss was a sweet lingering farewell to an enchanted moment of stolen happiness. There was no need for words.

We both knew that he would keep the promise he had made "in a welter of blood and tears" and I, though my heart might be broken, would never try to separate him from his wife and little son.

We left the darkness of the pavilion and stood on the lawn, reluctant to walk ahead into the glare of the headlights and join Abby and the men grouped beside the jeep. The little moon disappeared behind a cloud and the night was steeped in silence. Suddenly something stirred in the stillness. It was the merest whisper of sound but so close nearby that we both turned and looked back at the pavilion. I saw and recognized the figure that stood pressed against the metal pole that supported one corner of the awning.

I spoke sharply. "Delfina! What are you doing there?"

She took a step toward us. "I came with a tray for the glasses and the ashtrays. I see two people leave the pavilion and I wait here until they go where Darwin waits for them."

How long had she been standing there? What had she overheard or seen? With an effort I kept my voice steady as I said, "You may take them now."

Her answer was polite but her voice was sullen. "Thank you. Good night, Miss Alix. Good night, sir."

She did not move to enter the pavilion and as we walked across the lawn I was certain that she was watching us.

When the men left in the jeep with Darwin, Abby and I returned to the pavilion and sat in the darkness watching until far below us the dock appeared in the beam of the headlights. Four figures moved to the small boat moored alongside it. As the last one prepared to step down into it he turned and raised his arm in a final gesture of farewell.

"Dear Jens," said Abby, "he never forgets. I feel a little more lonely each time he leaves."

I slipped my arm around her.

"There's always a tomorrow," I reminded her.

In the dawn of the that night's tomorrow, as I stood at Claire's window in the tower, I remembered those words. For Abby, yes, there would be many tomorrows and many hours to spend contentedly with Jens but for me there were no tomorrows to be shared with Mark.

I went to the dining room, but since Abby was not

there I filled a small coffee pot from the percolator, put it on a tray with a cup and saucer and carried it to the library. My book about the Pompineaus was nearing completion but in my heart I knew I would never let it leave my hands for publication. Let the dead past bury its dead—I would not drag the corpses from their graves to satisfy the curiosity of a scandal-loving public.

I drank my coffee and fell to wondering about the little slave boy, Bozo, who had grown up in this house as the playmate of my great-grandfather. I had seen him stand before the wicked Jacques Pompineau in this very room and heard him speak the words "I obey." He had placed his hand on the writing table there, where now, the sun, striking through the window made a little pool of golden light.

No, not the sun. The light fell from a lighted lamp and was not golden but red as it struck through a crystal decanter of ruby-colored wine. The long, black fingers lay spread upon it like a pattern cut from black cardboard.

On the opposite side of the table Jacques Pompineau sat sprawled in a chair, his head with its mop of auburn curls sunk on the lace-edged frills of his shirt. He did not look up as Bozo left the room with the empty decanter and the other one from which only one drink had been poured. Nor did he look up when Bozo returned and placed a full decanter within easy reach of the shrunken figure in the chair. I watched with pity as the black man stooped and lifted the slender body of Claire, holding her like a child who had fallen asleep in his arms.

Time passed in the way it does in dreams, leaving no impression of its swift passage.

The decanter was empty. Jacques lay limp in his chair, a wine glass overturned on his chest, the spilled contents soaking into the satin and the frills that had been white. I had not seen Bozo re-enter the room but he was there looking down on Jacques, his features distorted with hatred. A bulging sack was slung over one shoulder; a long string of pearls dangled from a pocket. He put the sack on the floor and with both hands tore the ruby ring from Jacques' finger. A low moan came from the lips of the unconscious man.

Bozo flung the sack over his shoulders, opened the French door and walked out into the night.

In the room no sign remained of all that I had witnessed. The top of the writing table was bare except for a crystal vase filled with flowers freshly picked that morning before either Abby or I had wakened. The lighted lamp and the decanter of drugged wine had vanished and in the chair beside the table Jacques no longer sat and moaned in his sleep.

Chapter 15

Mark's phone call from St. Croix came a week later.
"Alix? This is Mark."
My voice which had answered the ring in a perfectly normal manner now stuck in my throat and emerged as a whisper.
"Good morning, Mark."
Will it always be like this when I hear his voice, I wondered. Then came the relieving thought, "Of course not. Nowadays women don't pine away for love."
Mark was saying, "I must see you, Alix. It's important. If I fly over now will you meet me in town for lunch?"
"Yes, I'd like to." My voice was steady again—I was glad to have it back. "Where shall we meet?"
"Will Hotel Eighteen twenty-five at one o'clock be convenient?"
"Yes, I can be there."
"Fine. I'll call Miss Gussie and tell her to expect us. Until one, then Alix."
"Until one."
I hung up the receiver and went back to the library to put away my manuscript and reference material. I thought Mark's choice of a meeting place a little odd because Miss Gussie, I knew, did not serve luncheon for guests. Maybe

he wanted to ensure that we would not be seen together in public. Was he afraid that Linda would hear of it and be jealous? She looked like the type who would make a scene over her husband's taking another woman to lunch. Was Mark so weak that he dared not offend her? I rejected that thought indignantly. Impossible! Not Mark. Still, I did not like the suggestion of a hole-in-the-corner rendezvous that had come to my mind. Better not to think about it. Just keep the appointment and let Mark explain.

As I started up the steep steps of the hotel I saw Miss Gussie at the top waiting for me.

"Come inside where it's cool." She took my hand and drew me with her into the combination dining room and bar. "Mark should be here any minute now and lunch will be ready as soon as you've had your drinks. Mark likes my martinis. My first husband taught me how to make them just right—he put the vermouth in with an eye dropper. He may have been a sleight-of-hand performer on the cash register but he never short-changed a customer with a poor martini. Mark even recommended him to his own guests."

"You've known Mark a long time, then?"

"Hell, yes. My ex-number-one and I had a little drive-in on St. Croix when Mark came there after his father's death. Jerry, his younger brother, was a swell kid—used to call me Auntie-Mom. Mark always drops in when he's here in town and lets me fix him a special lunch. Speaking of angels, here he comes and I haven't even asked you to sit down."

A car door slammed, there was a cheery whistle on the stairs and Mark's voice calling "You here, Miss Gussie? Our company arrive yet?"

He stood in the doorway and as he saw me, he stepped inside the room and took both my hands, holding them closely and smiling down at me. The scar was very white against his tanned cheek.

"I almost had to steal a car to get here," he laughed. "A bunch of Puerto Rican tourists grabbed the last taxi at the airport. None other than the Government Secretary gave me a lift."

Miss Gussie was at the bar stirring a pitcher of martinis. She set three glasses on the counter and filled them.

"I'll have one with you and then I'll be off to check

your lunch. Will you have it here or out on the gallery?"

"On the gallery, I think. That okay with you, Alix?"

"Very okay!" I said.

Certainly there was no hint of a hole-in-the-wall rendezvous on an open-air gallery in full daylight.

The lunch was brought by a smiling young native boy with a napkin hung over his starched white linen sleeve that constantly got in his way. There was cold vichyssoise in Royal Worcester cups, plump Cornish hens, a corn soufflé, hot buttered rolls fresh from the oven, sliced tomatoes and avocados and a lovely white wine. I kept wondering when Mark was going to tell me why he had stressed the importance of seeing me today, but it was only after we had left the table and settled ourselves in comfortable chairs in a vine-screened corner of the gallery that he gave me the reason. He spoke earnestly and with a tenseness that indicated carefully repressed emotion.

"I asked you to come here, Alix, to listen to a story. You don't have to listen. All you need to say is that you do not love me and the story will remain untold."

"I love you, Mark," I said.

He lit a cigarette and immediately crushed it out in an ashtray. "Then it's not only right but absolutely necessary that you hear what must be said."

"I will listen," I promised.

"There is a preface to the story and one day there will be an epilogue. In this preface a question is asked and an answer given. Will you marry me, Alix, when I can come to you honorably free to claim you?"

"I will," I said.

I put my hand in his and he raised it to his lips. We had exchanged our vows in this vine-shaded corner of the gallery as solemnly as if in the sanctity of a church. Nothing in Mark's story could sway my belief in his integrity.

"Ten years ago," he said, "when I inherited Le Sucrier from my father, I was twenty-three years old and my brother, Jerry, was eighteen. Our mother died when he was born and I took my responsibility as older brother very seriously. We had always been close and so I was worried when, that first summer at Le Sucrier, he got in with a lot of wild kids and started drinking in a big way. One day I discovered that he and his crowd were experimenting with drugs. He hated my knowing about it and respected me enough to give me his word he'd give it up. I believed him and I still believe that he would have kept his promise if Linda hadn't used every trick in the book to destroy his morale. One rainy night they went out in his car and on a bad stretch of road she told him she was pregnant and he would have to help her get rid of the child. He was shocked and scared and lost control of the car. The road was slick with rain: the car skidded and overturned. Linda managed to get out but Jerry was pinned in the wreckage. I had been visiting friends and was driving home slowly because of the rain. I took a short-cut on a back road and came on the scene of the accident only a few minutes after it had happened. I got Jerry out of the wreck . . ." He paused and closed his eyes and involuntarily, it seemed, his hand touched the scar on his cheek. "I'm sorry," he said after a moment. "I can't forget. It was too late to save him. I held him in my arms and just before he died he whispered, 'Protect Linda. My child—keep him. Promise.' I put him in my car before I drove to the hospital I took Linda to Miss Gussie who patched up her cuts and dragged the whole story out of her. Linda's father was here in St. Sebastian at the time, so Miss Gussie gave out a story of a virus infection and the need for rest and quiet. She is the only one who has ever known that Linda was in the car with Jerry that night."

He stood up and walked to the edge of the gallery. I sensed that in his thoughts he was reliving the terrible hours that had followed the tragedy. I waited quietly and when a few minutes had passed he came and stood in front of me, looking down into my face.

"I married her. I hated her, but it was the only way I could keep her from killing his child. It was an easy way out for her and she took it. We went abroad until the child was born. I adopted him as my own son. I offer no excuse for what followed. Even my love for Jerry did not warrant what I have done. For six years I have humiliated Linda by refusing to touch her. In public I have mocked her by acting the devoted husband. I have tolerated her only because of my promise to Jerry and the fact that Jimmy adores her. She either overindulges him or neglects him for days on end—it makes no difference: in his eyes she is perfect. I do not want him to know her as she is, selfish, greedy for money and attention, a borderline alcoholic, until he is old enough and wise enough to know how to pity instead of condemn.

"I have told you all this because I am ashamed. I have let you believe that I am a decent human being worthy of respect and love; I am worthy of neither. I have betrayed my brother's trust by hating when I should have pitied and tearing down, when I should have been building up, the moral strength of the one I had promised to protect. It is a terrible thing to live with hate. It makes a man despise himself. It eats away like acid and destroys both the one who hates and the one who knows he is hated."

My father had said, "It is not a good thing to live with fear." I had seen what it had done to him and how it had deprived me of the security and warmth of the love I needed. How much more devastating it would be to live with hate!

"It's gone now," Mark said, "all the hate and the passionate will to make her suffer."

He sat down and passed his hand over his forehead as if to rub out the bitter memories. He said, "Little by little, my love, for you drove the hate out of me. I began to love the simple little things in life like waking up to a new day, or tasting the sweetness of sugar from the cane in my own fields, the everyday things I'd always taken for granted. And then it came to me that the reason the whole world was beautiful was because you were in it. There was no room for hate in that world, Alix, no room at all. I began to think of ways I could help Linda make a new life for herself—her own home wherever she chooses to live, financial security, an equal share with me in the joy and responsibility of raising Jimmy. She has never liked Le Sucrier; she will be glad to be free of it. After the flurry and fuss of the ball is over I shall tell her that she will never be hurt again by my obsession with a promise that I have kept so badly.

"And some day, Alix, if you haven't grown tired of waiting for all the wrongs to be righted, will you let me ask my question again? Will your answer be the same?"

I put out my hand and touched the scar on his cheek, tracing the thin, white line with my fingertips.

"It will be the same, my love," I said.

Chapter 16

For our convenience it had been arranged that Abby, Jens, Jon, Miss Gussie and I should stay at Le Sucrier as Mark's guests for the ball. We arrived after lunch and were immediately caught up in the excitement that leaped like sparks between guests and employees alike. Red and white marquees had been set up on the lawn and strings of fairy lights festooned the trees and tall shrubs.

Mark came to greet us, looking young and carefree in white slacks, sport shirt and tennis shoes. A lock of hair hung down on his forehead and his cowlick stood on end as if powered by electricity.

"Linda's at the beach," he apologized. "All the hustle and bustle gave her a headache but she'll be back before long. We're having an early dinner so that everyone will have plenty of time to change into costume. Your bags will be in your rooms, but right now I want to take you back into another century."

He held the screen door open with a flourish and chuckled his appreciation of our amazement. The long corridor stretching from the front to the back of the house had been cleared of the plantation home furnishings that had been there on my previous visit. The light bulbs in the elaborate crystal chandelier had been replaced by candles, and the antique gold sconces fixed to the walls were reflected in old-fashioned mirrors hung opposite them. The woven straw hall runner was gone and the wood floor was glossy with wax. The doors to the double drawing room stood open and what had once been a typical West Indian parlor was revealed as an ivory and gold ballroom with four gilded chandeliers sparkling with crystal pendants and filled with dozens of white candles. The floor, with its inlaid pattern of fleur-de-lis, gleamed like satin, and at the far end of the room near the door to the garden a gilded shell had been erected for the musicians. On the wall opposite the doorway in which we were standing a garland of red and white carnations had been hung above a bank of palms in gilded pots.

"That's where the receiving line will stand," explained Mark, "with the birthday girl in the middle. Claire's brother, of whom very little is known, except that he was a disagreeable, dissipated character, will not be in the line but will wander about drunkenly. One of the guests, a young television actor here on vacation will portray him. Over there in that corner, there will be a table holding gifts supposed to have been sent to Claire for her birthday." With a twinkle in his eyes he added, "I'm afraid Alix will not admire my selection of junk jewelry."

"I've brought just the thing to put them in," I said. "It seemed to me that one of the gifts actually received by the real Claire on her birthday would give some authenticity to the party so I brought the jewel box which is said to have been given to her by Bozo."

Mark smiled at me. "Perhaps the little ghost will come in from the garden to admire it. We must watch for her."

Linda did not put in an appearance until the cocktail hour. She was very quiet, not exactly ungracious but close to it. Once I overheard her say airily to one of the hotel guests, "My costume? Oh, nothing special. Since I am only an extra in Mark's epic production I can hardly expect to be noticed."

"There!" I thought with annoyance. "I knew she'd be offended when Mark didn't insist that she play Claire. I shouldn't have let him persuade me to take the part."

During dinner she was pointedly rude to me and it was a relief when she left the table without waiting for coffee.

"I've a headache," she said shortly and added a begrudging, "see you later."

Mark tried to pass off her rudeness with the rueful apology that "Linda's headaches simply drive her up the wall," but our high spirits had been dampened by her overt hostility.

All the guests had been requested to arrive at nine o'clock in order to be present for the entrance of the governor and his official party and by eight-thirty Jon and I were ready to take our places in front of the palms. Jon made a magnificently pompous Jacques with his wig of auburn curls, his white silk suit with lace at his throat and wrists. As an added touch which I knew to be authentic I had bought a costume jewelry ring with a large red stone for him to wear on his forefinger. With an eyebrow pencil Abby had sketched lines on his face that added years to his appearance, and the resemblance to the Jacques I had seen in the terrible visions was so remarkable that I even felt a little uneasy standing beside him.

I doubted a little whether I, at twenty-two, could give a convincing performance of a radiant sixteen-year-old girl, the center of attraction at her first ball. The dress was right, the exact copy of one I'd found in Claire's wardrobe, white silk with a wide ruffled skirt worn over a crinoline and trimmed with small red velvet bows, but I knew that I lacked the naiveté of a very young girl as yet untouched by love.

I entered the ballroom and went to place the jewelry box among the other birthday gifts. Displayed with them was an old-fashioned bouquet of red and white rosebuds in a lace paper frill, tied with long streamers of narrow white satin ribbon. There was no card but I felt sure that Mark had put them there for me. A glance at my reflection in a mirror told me that no play-acting would be necessary that evening for I was, in effect, the embodiment of Claire.

At nine-thirty, heralded by the Danish national anthem, Jens, as the governor, made his appearance with Mark as Knud Jensen in attendance, followed by the members of his staff and their ladies.

I suppose that everyone at sometime in his life has used the expression "My heart stood still" to describe the effect of an overpowering emotion. I know that mine did later that evening when Mark, a romantic figure in his gold-braided white uniform, bowed before me and requested the honor of a dance. I went into his arms not as Alix Bonney masquerading as a girl falling in love, but as Claire Pompineau reincarnated for this one breathless moment in time.

It was during the intermission set aside for Claire to open her gifts that the mishap occurred that was to become the prelude to tragedy.

I had unwrapped all the packages, delighted by Mark's ingenuity in producing such a variety of inexpensive trifles to simulate the adornments fancied by the ladies of the last century, and had picked up the jewelry box which I had left to the last when the actor, who was impersonating Claire's brother too enthusiastically, lurched against me and knocked the box out of my hands. As it struck the table the top flew open and the blue velvet pad fell out, exposing the fleur-de-lis inlaid in the wood beneath it. Linda, who was near me, picked up the box and ran her finger over the design.

"That's odd," she said, "there's one just like this in—" then bit her lip and shut the box quickly, but not before I had seen that the central leaf of the trefoil was truncated at the tip. In a flashback of memory I saw myself with Jon in Claire's room examining the box and its modest contents. He had lifted a corner of the velvet pad and I had seen for the first and until just now the last time, the fleur-de-lis inlaid beneath it, yet strangely I had not noticed the defect in the design.

Linda was turning away with the box still in her hands when Miss Gussie stopped her with one of her little bird's claw hands.

"You'll tear your dress," she said. "You've caught the lace on a rough place."

Linda pulled away impatiently. "I don't need your help. I'll fix it myself."

She shook off Miss Gussie's arm and almost ran from the room.

Miss Gussie sniffed. "Well! You'd have thought I was about to tear her dress off her back! What was in the box, Alix?"

"Nothing but another fleur-de-lis in the wood."

"So what's so damned odd about that? Don't tell me she

never saw one before with a whole slew of them here right under her feet."

I smiled, but the incident troubled me. My mind bombarded me with questions. Would a skilled craftsman like Bozo have been likely to fashion a defective design in a gift intended for Claire? And what was even more improbable, would he have left a rough place in the wood on which she could hurt her finger? Where had Linda seen another fleur-de-lis with a truncated leaf? And why had she been in such a hurry to hide it from sight?

The intermission came to an end and as the musicians played the first strains of a waltz Jon came to claim me for the dance.

"I'm weary of looking daggers at your patterns," he said, "How about letting your pseudo-father dance with the prettiest girl at the ball?"

As we circled the floor, nodding and smiling at the guests, I asked, "When we opened Claire's room and found the jewelry box did you notice anything unusual about it—the box, I mean?"

"No, I can't say I did. Was there?"

"Linda seemed to think so just now. Some threads of her dress caught in the fleur-de-lis under the velvet and before she ran off with it I saw that one leaf was different from the others. I wonder how we both happened to miss that?"

"I don't think we looked at it very closely."

"We didn't. I got a little teary and we put the box away. I never looked inside it again until this morning when I took Claire's jewelry out and put it away. I didn't move the pad."

"Did Linda say anything?"

"Yes. She said, 'That's odd. There's one just like this in—' and then she slammed the lid down."

"And, you say, went away with it. Well, what you've got to do is get it back as soon as you can. Tell her it belongs to the historical society and you're responsible for it. Tell her anything, but get it away from her. I want a look at that fleur-de-lis."

My curiosity, already aroused by Linda's strange behavior, detected the not of urgency in his voice.

"I'll do it now," I said.

We were near the hall door so I slipped away from him

141

and went in search of Linda. I could not find her anywhere. In fact she did not appear until much later when the buffet supper was served.

I was seated between Jens who, as governor, had taken me in, and Mark, who had escorted Abby. At a nearby table Linda talked with animation to Darcy and ignored Jon who was at her other side. Laughing, Darcy raised his wine glass to his lips and I saw the great ruby that had belonged to Jacques glowing in the ring on his finger.

I had last seen that ring when Bozo, a string of pearls hanging out of his pocket, had bent over the unconscious form of his master and removed the ring from his finger.

One more proof, I thought, that Darcy was the descendant of a humble slave, and not, as he claimed, of Louis Pompineau—a proof that I could not use, for who would believe that I had actually seen visions of past events?

There were to be fireworks on the lawn, so after the supper Abby and I collected our beaded silk reticules, our lace fans, and long white kid gloves and with Jens and Mark mingled with the others in the corridor who were on their way to watch the display. Ahead I could see Jon, his curly auburn wig a trifle askew as he bent his head and spoke to the couples as they passed. He must have sensed that I was watching him for he looked about and as his eyes found me he grinned and flicked an eyelid in an almost imperceptible wink.

In one of the mirrors on the wall I caught a glimpse of Linda running swiftly up the stairs, her voluminous organdy skirt swaying like a bell suspended from her slender waist. She looked back once over her shoulder as if she thought someone was behind her on the stairs and then ran on. I thought there was something odd, almost furtive in her haste, but the impression was only fleeting and I thought no more about it.

As Mark and I walked out of the house onto the moonlit lawn he touched my arm and said, "Let's take a look in the garden now that probably no one is there and see if the little ghost has come to her birthday party."

So we walked around the side of the house, past the brightly lighted windows of the empty ballroom and into the garden just as the first rocket burst in a shower of silver stars.

Chapter 17

The air was sweet with the fragrance of jasmine. Flower beds in a variety of shapes bloomed with lilies and geraniums and roses. Glossy-leaved bushes loaded with gardenias, massed against a low brick wall, vied in fragrance with the jasmine that seemed to be everywhere.

In the center of the garden at the intersection of two paths bordered with zinnias and marigolds, was a marble bench beneath an arbor of climbing roses. Without a word Mark and I walked to it, the white, crushed coral on the path scrunching under our feet and glistening in the light of the rockets exploding overhead. We sat quietly watching for the little ghost that was dear to us both.

She came, walking among the flowers, stooping to touch a rose or pick a spray of jasmine to put in her hair. Her dress was the color of moonlight and her bare shoulders were as white as the petals of the rose she had tucked in the lace on her low-cut bodice.

Mark put his face close to mine and whispered, "Look! There by the big tree."

Out from the shadow of an ancient mahogany tree stepped another, taller figure with hair the color of the gold braid on the white uniform he was wearing. He held out his arms and Claire ran to him like a white moth in the darkness.

They walked as lovers do, his arm around her waist, her head not quite reaching his shoulder, resting in the curve of his arm. They came to the arbor, and as they passed by, a spray of jasmine fell from her hand into my lap. I looked down at it, hardly able to believe that the little froth of star-flowers was real and not just something I had imagined. I picked it up and drew it across my face—it was living and fresh and fragrant.

I looked for the lovers but they were gone.

Someone came out of the garden door in the back drawing room and hurried up the path to the arbor. His auburn curls bobbed on the shoulders of his white coat as he broke into a run.

"Mark, are you here?" he called.

Mark stepped out into the moonlight. "What is it, Jon? Am I needed?"

"It's Linda. She's been hurt—I don't know how badly."

Without hesitation I went with them, running to keep up with their long strides. The back drawing room was empty and the door to the corridor had been closed. As we went into the front half of the big double room I stopped, unable to move, transfixed by the sight of a great hole in the floor immediately in front of where I had stood, earlier, in the receiving line. Mark and Jon went to the edge of the hole and peered down into it. Sick with fear I followed.

A section of the floor had been raised on hinges. Beneath it an ordinary trap door fitted with a bolt and a long chain hung down into the hole. A flight of shallow stone steps led down to a stone-paved floor. And on that floor, shrouded in the organdy and lace folds of her ball gown, lay Linda, her arms outflung, a broken flashlight lying just beyond her fingers, her neck twisted at an impossible angle so that she seemed to be looking at us from between her shoulders. I shuddered, and as Jon's arm went around me for support I buried my face in his shoulder.

Mark was already on the steps. "Get Jens," he said, "and keep everyone out of here."

While Jon was gone I stood in the corridor with my back against the ballroom door and tried to keep my voice steady as I repeated over and over "There's been an accident. Please remain outdoors for the present." I made no attempt to reply to the storm of questions that followed—it would have been impossible for me to speak of the terrible thing that had happened.

When Jon returned he brought with him not only Jens but Abby as well and a doctor who was one of the many guests from St. Sebastian. Abby drew me into the room with her and shut and locked the door.

"Miss Gussie is asking everyone to leave quietly," she said. "Is Linda badly hurt?"

I clenched my teeth to stop their chattering. "I'm afraid, oh, Abby, it's terrible—I think she's dead."

Mark called up from below: "There are flashlights in the closet by the garden door. Bring them down with you."

Abby and I went first and stood at the foot of the steps training the beams of our flashlights on Linda while the doctor knelt at Mark's side and examined Linda's body.

"I'm sorry, Mark. Linda is dead. Her neck was broken in a fall down the stairs."

He pointed to a satin slipper with an exaggeratedly high heel that was lying on one of the steps. "She may have turned her ankle and there was nothing for her to catch hold of."

They carried her up the steps and we covered her with some smocks that we found hanging in the closet.

Mark stood looking down at the woman he had once hated. Then he stooped and brushed back a lock of her hair that had fallen over her eyes. I heard him whisper, "Poor Linda. It's too late. Now you'll never know that I'm sorry."

Yes, poor Linda, who would never know that she was free of the hatred she had endured so many years. Poor Mark, too, who would never forget that he had waited too long to tell her of her release.

I went and stood at the edge of the gaping hole and tried to imagine Linda's excitement when she had started down into the darkness where a treasure might be awaiting discovery. And there had been nothing there. I had flashed the torch around the bare room and had seen nothing but some heavy chains fixed to the walls. Had it been a place of punishment for rebellious slaves? For this—for nothingness—she had lost her life. She had waited until the house was empty, when even the servants were outdoors watching the fireworks, and had gone to the ballroom to find the treasure by herself.

On the floor beside my foot lay Claire's jewelry box. I picked it up and saw that the fleur-de-lis with the blunted leaf had been prised up and, with the wooden peg on which it was mounted, formed a handle to lift the lid of a secret compartment. Linda had been quick to grasp the significance of the truncated leaf of the fleur-de-lis. "There is one just like it in . . ." she had said and holding the box against her had run from the room.

I looked for the instrument she had used to prise up the parquetry inlay and found a paper knife with a thin blade that could slip easily into the smoothly finished edges of the fleur-de-lis.

Linda had been mistaken. There was no treasure in the dungeon here at Le Sucrier. Did it lie, then, beneath the floor of some room in the chateau—a room with a window through which I had seen pirates disappear, laden with sacks of loot? A room where Bozo could have disposed quickly of two bodies and returned to strip the unconscious Jacques of his ruby ring?

I lowered the door so that it covered the hole and examined the chunk of polished wood shaped like a fleur-de-lis with a blunted leaf that protruded on a steel rod from the center of the door. I closed my hand around it and pulled: the door came up easily.

Suddenly I was aware of eyes fixed on me from across the room. I raised my head and saw a face staring in through an open window partially screened by the potted palms.

Darcy! Darcy who had searched the chateau by night for the fabulous treasure that was said to be there. Darcy who had tried unsuccessfully to kill me because I stood in the way of his false claim to an enormous inheritance. Darcy who now knew what to look for in the chateau and how to gain access to the hidden room.

I could not tear my eyes from his face, that handsome mask of a conniver, a cheat, an interloper and, yes, a murderer, although the only proof of that was my vision of Brandish's death at his hands—and who, in this age of reason based on cold facts, believes in anything as fantastic as a vision?

He looked straight at me and I saw his expression of triumph. The next instant he was gone and only the movement of a few leaves of palm betrayed that he had been there.

"Jon!" I exclaimed sharply.

He came to me quickly. "What is it, Alix? You look frightened."

"I am. Jon, we must go to the chateau at once. Darcy was there at that window—I saw him. I don't know how long he'd been there but it was long enough for him to see how to locate a secret room. He'll go to the chateau as quickly as he can. We've got to get there first—Jon, we've got to!"

"Good Lord! Are you sure it was Darcy you saw?"

"I'm positive. What are we going to do? The first Goose won't leave for ages yet. Could we get to the airport and charter a small plane?"

"Not at this hour—it isn't dawn yet. Wait!" He snapped his fingers. "The 'copter! Go tell Jens; he can explain to Mark later. Meet me out back—and hurry!"

I found Jens at the telephone with Abby. "He's talking to Linda's father," she said.

I gave her my message and she nodded agreement. "Go quickly. Jens and I are staying with Mark for as long as we can be of help. Ask Jon to stay with you until we get back—I don't want you to be alone in the house."

I ran out by the garden door. No one was in sight as I raced to where Jon was waiting at the helicopter. As we rose off the ground I noticed that the sky was pink with the coming of dawn. To steady my hands that were trembling I tried to grip them together and found to my surprise that they still held the jewelry box that I had unconsciously brought with me. I took hold of the little handle and pulled up the lid to the false bottom. Inside there was a slip of paper marked with deep yellow creases. It had been unfolded and then doubled over without regard to the age-old creases and had been jammed into the box so carelessly that the brittle paper had torn in several places. I strained my eyes to read the words written in ink that had faded over the years.

"Miss Claire:

When I showed you this morning, your birthday, how to open this secret compartment I did not tell you about the

147

note I was going to put here for you to find some day. Never let your father handle this box or see the note—my life would be forfeit. The location of a room filled with treasure is a secret known only to the males of the Pompineau family and to me who was trusted to design a new way to disguise the entrance. Some day you may want to escape this prison in which your father is determined to keep you all your life. When that day comes look for a fleur-de-lis with a leaf broken off at the tip—you will know what to do with it. Guard this secret as you would your life that of your devoted servant, Bozo."

As I was reading the last words Jon touched my arm and pointed to the lazy outline of Mon Domaine.

"Can I land there?" he shouted.

"Yes, at the back."

I gave him the letter and while he read it I watched the sky as anxiously as if it had been a four-lane highway packed with traffic.

"Relax," I told myself.

Jon brought the helicopter down in the field near the coach house. Darwin came to the door, rubbing his eyes. When he saw me he grinned and went back to his interrupted sleep.

I had been afraid that we might have to break a louver at one of the windows to get in the house but the door to the rear loggia had been left unlocked. It seemed to be a habit of Delfina's to leave doors open that should be locked!

We ran down the west arcade to the foyer in the tower and threw open the door to the library. Feverishly eager, we dragged the furniture to the center of the room and rolled back the heavy rug. A half hour later we sat back on our heels and looked at each other miserably.

"It was the logical place to look," I moaned. "Oh, the time that we've wasted!"

"How about the foyer?"

"I doubt it, but we can try."

We didn't even need to move the console table, and the oriental rug was easy to move. And there it was, the fleur-de-lis with the broken leaf!

I rushed to the library and snatched up a paper knife from the table. Kneeling, I thrust the point into the almost invisible crack between the inlay and the three-foot square of polished wood in which it was centered. With nearly unbearable suspense I increased the pressure and levered the inlay up until I could grasp it with my fingers.

"Pull!" urged Jon. "For heavens' sake, pull!"

I dropped my hands and looked at him helplessly.

"I can't," I said. "You do it."

The door came up smoothly. Beneath it was a heavy wooden door with a long chain attached. As Jon picked up the chain I scrambled to my feet and took it from him.

"Let me do it," I said, and pulled, praying foolishly that the heavy, forged links would not part before the door was raised.

As it moved upward the stairs came into view, stone, hollowed by the passage of many feet long since at rest.

"Come," said Jon and gave me his hand.

Chapter 18

The surface of the steps was uneven and there were no handrails at the sides. Remembering Linda's high-heeled slipper lying on the dungeon steps at Le Sucrier I sat down and removed mine while Jon directed the beam of his flashlight into the dark void at the foot of the steps.

"We're going to need more light than this," he said. "I've got a feeling that this room is a lot bigger than the one at Mark's."

"There's a supply of battery-operated storm lanterns in the service room."

"Where's that?"

"Opposite here on the other arcade. I'll get them."

"No, we'll go together."

"But shouldn't one of us stay here?"

"We both should, but since that's impossible we'll both go get the lanterns. It's not safe for you alone."

"There's no one in the house."

"I hope you're right. But there's something here. I can feel it and I don't like it. Come on."

Jon was right. There was something in the house, something ancient and evil and menacing. It went with us across the loggia and into the storeroom and seemed to press closer as we hurried back, each carrying two lanterns and a few extra batteries we'd found on a shelf.

My slippers and Claire's jewelry box were still on the step where I'd left them. It was oddly reassuring to find them there.

In the harsh white light of the powerful lanterns the vast repository of the Pompineau treasure looked disappointingly like an ordinary storeroom filled with an accumulation of odds and ends. There were tables and sideboards, beds with massive, carved headboards and chairs of every size and description, from great, thronelike seats to dainty little chairs fit for a queen's boudoir. And, aligned against one long wall like orderly graves in a cemetery were chests, some carved, some unadorned, some that had once been polished, some mere slabs of wood nailed together like rough coffins.

"The treasure," breathed Jon.

We started together for the chests but Jon was quicker than I. I saw him raise the lid of one and heard him whistle as he peered into it.

"There's a fortune in this one alone," he said in awed tones.

I dropped to my knees on the gritty floor and dipped my hands into the heap of rainbow-colored jewels that lay just as they had been thrown or dumped from sacks into the deep chest. There were ropes and chokers of pearls and chains of diamonds set in gold. There were brooches and bracelets and circlets and rings in dazzling confusion.

"My God," said Jon over and over, and then, "I don't believe it. It can't be true, Alix."

Something had caught my eye. I pulled myself to my feet and pointed excitedly to a wisp of ragged, faintly pink silk hanging from under the lid of the chest that stood nearest the door. I literally threw myself at it, and hampered by my long, voluminous skirt stumbled and would have fallen if Jon had not flung out his arm to steady me.

"Steady there," he said. "I'll open it."

The lid came up slowly—grudgingly, I thought—revealing the pitiful remains of the lovers, little more than the shreds of a pink lace gown and a white uniform trimmed with tarnished gold braid. They lay on a pile of church vestments that had once been gorgeous—white, red, purple, gold, black, green, crusted with gold embroidery.

My eyes stung with sudden tears. I could not bear to look at the mute testimony of man's violence, cowardice and fear. My knees felt as if they would give way under me—I turned blindly toward the stairs.

"Very touching," said a voice above me.

I jerked my head up and cried out in alarm.

André Darcy stood half-way down the flight of stairs, a smile of derision on his lips, and in his hand, pointing at me, was a gun. Behind him, on the step above, stood Delfina, her black eyes blazing with triumph.

"Don't move, either of you," he said. "Delfina is going to tie you up nice and tight, and we are going to have quite a talk—a good, long talk since your friends won't be coming back for a day or two. Okay, Delfina. Don't be afraid to use plenty of rope. There seems to be a lot more in the store room."

He dragged two chairs from the piles of furniture and set them beside each other facing the stairs. Holding the gun on us he waited until Delfina had bound us securely and cut the ends of the rope with a sharp knife that was thrust in the waistband of her skirt. Then he motioned to her to sit on the steps below him.

"You may thank me for not gagging you," he told us. "Scream if you wish, my dear Alix, but it will do you no good. Darwin and the Puerto Ricans are working too far off to hear you."

"You can't get away with this, you know," I said, my voice a lot steadier than my nerves.

"Hush!" Jon's voice was steady, like mine. "Let's hear what he has to say."

"I shan't be brief," jeered Darcy. "You're going to die—naturally that can't be helped—but there's no need for you to die of curiosity. First, how did I get here? I helped myself to Linda's car—she'd given me the keys a long time ago—and caught the first Goose. Came here in my own boat which I keep in the harbor. Next, where did I get the idea to pose as Louis Pompineau's great-grandson? From my great-grandfather, himself, no less. Of course he's been dead for a hell of a long time, but he'd made up a story about his life on an island in the Caribbean complete with descriptions of the chateau on it and the people who lived there but never told the name of the island or of the people he'd lived with. He described a room filled with pirate loot from which he had helped himself generously to finance his escape from the island, which he never explained, and to set himself up in business in a new place. There was a secret way to find the room in the chateau but he never told it. I've dreamed of the treasure ever since I first heard about it in a bedtime story and my mind had been made up to find it. Then one day I saw an ad in the paper about an island in the Caribbean named St. Sebastian. I put that together with the fact that my great-grandfather's name was Sebastian and took a gamble on the chance that there was a connection. I came secretly and when I saw the chateau I knew I had it made if I could find a way to get in and search for the treasure. I used to prowl around at night looking for a way to get in and one night I ran into Delfina. She joined forces with me for a share of the treasure if we could find it. Her stories of the family history gave me what I needed to impersonate an heir to the estate and the fortune. She was a great help."

Delfina tossed her head proudly. "André promised to get rid of Darwin and marry me as soon as he gets the chateau. Lord, how peoples will come whining to me for money and how quick I'll turn them down!"

Darcy almost choked on his laughter.

"What fools women are—all of them. Marry you, Delfina? When I can have my pick of the women who swarm around me begging for the favor of showering me with money and gifts? When even Mark Kitteredge's wife would have left him for me if I'd said the word?"

Delfina sprang at him, her fingers reaching for his face.

He shot her as coldbloodedly as he would have stamped on a cockroach. She fell backward and rolled to the floor where she lay motionless in a slowly widening pool of blood, the color of the gypsy-red skirt she wore.

"Now, where were we?" asked Darcy.

I glared at him with loathing. "You fiend! You unspeakable monster! You . . ."

Jon burst out with a torrent of epithets of which I could only guess the meaning.

Darcy scowled and leveled the gun at Jon's face. Then he shrugged. "Well, to resume. I wrote to Brandish and he granted me an interview. Oh, it was good that night! He'd been playing chess before Delfina let me in by the library window. There was a decanter of wine and two glasses on the table. Delfina had briefed me so well that he believed what I told him—everything—until I made my one mistake. Among my great-grandfather's possessions was a ruby ring in a setting of two gold fleur-de-lis." He held up his hand for us to see the ring on his finger. "To clinch my case, as I thought, I took this ring from my pocket and told him that my great-grandfather Louis had carried it away with him on the night he left the chateau forever. His face became livid and he screamed at me that the ring had belonged to Jacques and had been stolen from him by a runaway slave twenty years after Louis had left the island. He called me a liar and a cheat and I killed him. Delfina hid me in the fort until the excitement blew over. I still stay there sometimes as you discovered to your sorrow, didn't you, Alix? After awhile I made my appearance as a claimant to the estate. Nothing stands in my way now except you, whom I shall eliminate, and a question that I will be asked to answer. With all the research you have done on the Pompineaus you are sure to know what that question will be." He lowered the gun so that it pointed at my heart. "What is that question, Alix?"

"I don't know!" I cried, and added in a flash of bravado, "If I did I wouldn't tell you!"

He moved the gun up to the level of my face. "I think you could be persuaded."

"Why, if you're going to kill me anyway?"

"A little torture might make you change your mind. Lighted cigarettes applied with pressure are said to be very effective."

"I don't know! I don't know!" I repeated, trying to keep the rising hysteria out of my voice.

"Listen, you!" Jon's voice was a shout. I turned my head to look at him. He had stopped straining against the ropes and was attempting to divert Darcy's attention away from me. "If Alix says she doesn't know what the question is you can damn well believe her. I'll tell you something else: under torture she'd say the same thing. I can see why you think you have to kill us, but you don't really, you know. Now if I were in your place—you really haven't a ghost of a chance to get the inheritance, you know—I'd stuff a couple of suitcases full of these gorgeous jewels and get the hell out of here as fast and as far as I could. They say South America's the best place to hide out, but on the other hand . . ."

What in the world was the matter with Jon? He was actually babbling.

"Hold it," snapped Darcy.

He stood up and leveled the gun again at my heart.

"Any last words?" he asked.

I tipped my head back so that I could look him straight in the eye when he pulled the trigger. He might have the power to make me a corpse but not a coward.

Something hurled from the top of the stairs, landed on Darcy's back with crushing impact and plunged with him to the stone floor. The crack as Darcy's head hit, and the loud report as the gun went off sounded simultaneously.

Mark stood up and looked at me anxiously.

"Are you all right?" he asked.

I nodded and managed a smile.

"Thank God. When Abby told me she saw Darcy leave right after you and Jon, and said she was afraid you might be in danger, I couldn't let anything keep me from getting to you as fast as I could. My Skylane's always ready at the airport."

"And me, too, of course," quipped Jon.

Mark grinned at him. "Nothing like paying old debts. Knocked that character out cold, didn't I?"

"He isn't dead?" I asked. "That crack when his head hit the floor . . ." I broke off with a shudder.

"He'll live—he's breathing okay. We'll call an ambulance and the police as soon as I get you both unwound."

He bent over Delfina and took the knife from the waistband of her skirt. He felt for the pulse in her wrist and nodded confidently. "This one's going to be all right, too. She's lost a good bit of blood but the wound may be superficial."

While he slashed the ropes that bound me to the chair Jon asked him, "How long were you up there on the stairs? I saw you first when Darcy threatened Alix—you must have moved a little. I tried to stall Darcy but he wasn't having any of that."

Mark laughed. "I was there when you were scorching the air with that vocabulary we picked up in the army.

Since Darcy was in a confidential mood I decided not to interrupt—the more he talked the tighter he'd pull the noose around his neck. You okay, Alix? Good. Now for Jon. Call the hospital and the police and send Darwin to meet them at the waterfront."

"Wait!"

Delfina had opened her eyes and was struggling to support herself on her elbow.

"I been listening," she said, her voice surprisingly strong for one who had lost so much blood. "I ain't hurt bad— Darcy's a bungler. I even had to finish off Brandy for him. I'll put that noose around his neck for you. I'll tell everything."

"That won't be necessary," said Jon. "I've got it all down on tape."

It was raining—one of those torrential downpours that occur in the islands during the hurricane season. Huge drops, driven by fitful gusts of wind drummed against the windows of the library where Jens, Abby and I sat listening to dull, legal phrases pronounced by Attorney Tom Turner who had come to the chateau to spare me the discomfort of a trip across the harbor in such weather.

With maddening precision he slit the envelope Brandish Pompineau had left to be opened on this day and took from it a single sheet of paper folded in the middle. My hands were clammy and my mouth was dry as ashes. In another minute I would know which identity was to be mine for the future: Alix Pompineau, mistress of Mon Domaine and all the riches pertaining to it, or Alix Bonney, whose one material possession of any value was a modest, white-columned house at the end of an avenue of magnolias in the city of Augusta, Georgia. Yet even as I waited for that paper to be unfolded I shrank from the dreadful inheritance of ancient evil that might be mine.

Tom Turner turned back the fold of the paper and in a sonorous voice read the question that I must answer.

"What are the exact words of the Pompineau curse, known only to the Pompineaus, to call down perpetual evil upon their enemies or to annihilate them forever?"

I stood up and in a voice I hardly recognized as my own cried with a proud authority that was new to me, "Anathema Maranatha!"

Instantly a hush fell over the room followed by a great rush of turbulent sound that came out from the walls and filled the entire chateau with discordant shrieks of incoherent rage.

We sat with our hands over our ears shivering in the blasts of icy wind that accompanied the bedlam of maniacal howls.

Suddenly the air was warm and fresh as the earth scent of a garden after a gentle shower. Not a sound disturbed the stillness as peace flowed into every cranny of the ancient house haunted down the years by specters of an evil past.

With a surge of joy in my heart I knew that Claire, the gentle little ghost, and her lover were at rest forever.

The word, once spoken in wrath between brother and brother, had ceased at last to live, and with its death there was born for a new generation of Pompineaus the promise of a future unfettered by fear of its evil power.

⋽§ Epilogue §⋺

It is cool in the open court of the chateau and quiet except for the laughter of two small children who are sitting on the ledge of the pink marble fountain and dabbling their hands in the water to startle the goldfish that live there among the lily pads. Claire who is four and a coquette has put a sprig of jasmine in her auburn curls, but Mark who is two and of a more practical turn of mind is tearing the flowers off the sprig I have given him and is feeding them to the goldfish.

The tourists have gone back to their ships, most of them with a pamplet containing a short and glamorized history of the chateau and the early pirates who used to stand, spyglass in hand, looking out to sea from the windows of the observatory. They have stared in fascinated wonder at a roped-off area in which a square of parquet flooring has been removed to reveal a trap door and a flight of stone steps leading down to a treasure room from which the treasure has been removed to the more prosaic precincts of a bank.

Jens and Abby, most happily married, live in the chateau and supervise the teen-aged volunteers who guide the tourists through the chateau which is the pride of the

St. Sebastian Historical Society whom I have appointed as Guardians of the Estate.

Jon, the homesick Georgian, now owns and lives in the white-columned house at the end of an avenue of magnolias in Augusta, Georgia and when he is not busy at the TV station of which he is manager, grows the camelias he loves and observes the cardinals and mocking birds that flock to his garden. When asked if he would like to return to the noisy, exotic island of St. Sebastian he replies in the words of Miss Gussie, "Hell, no!"

Mark and I live at Le Sucrier. If the baby which is due to arrive at Easter is a girl her father insists that she be named Bonney Alix.

In our garden, near the arbor, is a bed of pink and white roses that bloom on a simple, unmarked grave of the two lovers who met and fell in love at Le Sucrier and walked in the garden together after death.

Jimmy, our dearly loved, red-haired, freckle-faced, eleven-year-old Number One Son spends many happy hours of each day with his grandfather, the judge, who is now retired and lives at Le Sucrier. He is mellowing slowly, like fine wine, and Jimmy adores him as he adored Linda.

Miss Gussie has heard from her recalcitrant third husband for whom, as I have suspected from the first, she carries a sizable torch.

Darcy and Delfina are serving long terms in a stateside penitentiary for the murder of Brandish Pompineau. The warden complains about the size of Darcy's fan mail from lady admirers.

Sometimes I stand in Abby's pavilion and look at the chateau, remembering how I first saw it in a painting I had found in an old trunk in the attic. I still think, as I did then, that I could look at it forever and not tire. It is lovely in the morning when the sun comes up over the hills and bathes it in golden light but I love it most when its walls are pink in the glow of sunset and the tree-frogs pipe their endless co-kee and in the garden, "Cum night de jasmun smell real purty."